He laug... made an unexpected happiness swell inside Sara.

Adam might not be Mr. Perfect Forever, but he was doing a pretty good job of being Mr. Perfect for Tonight. Despite the suit, his carefree beach attitude still cloaked him, and it tempted her to adopt it for herself, if only for a little while. She wondered what it was like to live a life so free from worry or responsibility.

"Do you always have this much fun?"

"I certainly try." He winked at her, which caused an odd, fluttery sensation to race across her skin.

Good thing he was only a "tonight" guy. He had a way of getting past her defenses and common sense, tempting her to think that things like responsibility and stability maybe didn't matter so much.

Dear Reader,

As a reader myself, I've always enjoyed series of books that return to the same setting for different stories. I love the feeling of getting to know not only a hero and heroine but also the friends, family and neighbors around them. Not to mention the town they call home. That's why I'm excited to be able to return to Horizon Beach, Florida, the setting of my first Harlequin American Romance, *A Firefighter in the Family*. But this time, Zac and Randi are happily married. Now it's Zac's best friend, laid-back Adam Canfield, who gets a second chance at love in *The Family Man*.

But Adam's not going down that road again willingly. He might seem to be carefree, but it takes a lot of work to hide the horror in his past that refuses to release its grip on him. The last thing he needs is to fall for Detective Sara Greene—a woman with not only a dangerous job but also two adopted daughters. Sara has the dream of creating the perfect family. She already has two beautiful kids. Now all she needs is the perfect guy. And Adam Canfield, with his lack of ambition and aversion to responsibility, certainly isn't Mr. Perfect. Or is he?

I hope you enjoy Adam and Sara's story. I always love to hear from readers, either via my Web site, www.trishmilburn.com, or my mailing address, P.O. Box 140875, Nashville, TN 37214-0875.

Trish Milburn

The Family Man
TRISH MILBURN

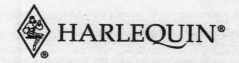

HARLEQUIN®

TORONTO • NEW YORK • LONDON
AMSTERDAM • PARIS • SYDNEY • HAMBURG
STOCKHOLM • ATHENS • TOKYO • MILAN • MADRID
PRAGUE • WARSAW • BUDAPEST • AUCKLAND

Recycling programs
for this product may
not exist in your area.

ISBN-13: 978-0-373-75304-8

THE FAMILY MAN

Printed in U.S.A.

ABOUT THE AUTHOR

Trish Milburn wrote her first book in the fifth grade and has the cardboard-and-fabric-bound, handwritten and colored-pencil-illustrated copy to prove it. That "book" was called *Land of the Misty Gems*, and not surprisingly it was a romance. She's always loved stories with happy endings, whether those stories come in the form of books, movies, TV programs or marriage to her own hero.

A print journalist by trade, she still does contract and freelance work in that field, balancing those duties with her dream-come-true career as a novelist. Before she published her first book, she was an eight-time finalist in the prestigious Golden Heart contest sponsored by Romance Writers of America, winning twice. Other than reading, Trish enjoys traveling (by car or train—she's a terra firma girl!), watching TV and movies, hiking, nature photography and visiting national parks.

You can visit Trish online at www.trishmilburn.com. Readers also can write to her at P.O. Box 140875, Nashville, TN 37214-0875.

Books by Trish Milburn

HARLEQUIN AMERICAN ROMANCE
1228—A FIREFIGHTER IN THE FAMILY
1260—HER VERY OWN FAMILY

To Shane, thanks for the support,
not minding my insane book collection,
and for agreeing to frequent takeout for dinner.

To Mary Fechter, thanks so much for your wonderful
friendship, and for the great compliment you gave
this book. I hope what you said comes true.

Again, I must thank my fabulous agent,
Michelle Grajkowski, and my wonderful editor,
Johanna Raisanen. Not only are you great career
partners, but you're also just fun to hang out with.

Chapter One

Sara Greene showed the snapshot to the landscaper preparing to mow the strip of grass between the back of the Sea Breeze Hotel and the beach. He examined the image of fourteen-year-old David Taylor then shook his head.

"Sorry, haven't seen him."

The same words she'd heard all morning—which meant she repeated herself as well when she handed the guy a business card.

"If you do see him, please give me a call."

Sara took a few steps down the wooden walkway over the sand before stopping, closing her eyes and lifting her face toward the bright Florida sky. It was as if the kid had gone poof and disappeared. She chose to think he was just really good at hiding because she didn't want to consider that he might have gotten himself into a dangerous or deadly situation.

One more long, deep breath of sea air was all she allowed herself before she opened her eyes and stared at the thatch-roofed beach bar beyond the ridge of dunes. She doubted David Taylor had been hanging out at the Beach Bum, but she was determined to check every possibility. Maybe one of the staff had spotted him elsewhere.

Only an older couple sat at the front edge of the open-sided bar, sipping what looked like lemonade as they watched the waves. After all, it was too early in the day to bring out the hard stuff. But from the sound of rattling bottles from behind the long wooden bar, someone was already at work.

"Hello?"

The hidden person clanked bottles a couple more times before he popped up from behind the bar like a jack-in-the-box clown. She recognized the tanned, lightly stubbled, handsome face of Adam Canfield, but she was used to it being on the customer side of the bar.

The bright smile, the one he used in his endless flirting with anyone with boobs, dimmed somewhat when he noticed it was her facing him.

"Hello, Detective." Adam shoved his hands in the back pockets of his khaki shorts. "Little early for a drink, isn't it?"

For the briefest moment, she missed him not flirting with her like he had the first time they'd met. He was the kind of man who could make a thrill zing along a woman's skin with a sexy look in those green eyes and thinly veiled suggestions. But he'd made it clear that her being a cop was a buzz-kill for him.

That was fine with her since she wasn't the least bit interested in a guy who went through life one or two steps above being a bum.

She pushed aside the temptation to fantasize and took a couple steps closer. "I'm still on duty."

"Zac's not here." He tossed an empty cardboard case in the trash can. "Please tell me someone hasn't cooked up some more bogus crap about him."

"This isn't about Mr. Parker, but nice conclusion-jumping." Zac Parker, owner of the Beach Bum, had been a potential suspect in a recent arson until the state arson investigator determined he was being set up. Then she ended up marrying him.

Adam raised a dark eyebrow at her snarky comment. She didn't acknowledge it, instead handed him the photo of David Taylor. "Have you seen this boy?"

While he looked at the snapshot of David in a school hallway, Suz Thackery came out of the storeroom behind him, her red hair piled atop her head in a loose twist, and glanced at the photo around his shoulder. To keep from looking at Adam, Sara focused on Suz.

Par for the course, they both shook their heads.

"He in some kind of trouble?" Suz asked.

"Ran away from home. Considering he's only fourteen, we're doing all we can to find him."

Adam looked at the photo again. "What's he running away from?"

Sara stared at him, at his sexy stubble and sandy brown, slightly messy hair—and wished she could look at him without noticing those attributes. Despite their mutual, if unvoiced, agreement that dating each other was not on the agenda, she couldn't help the way her pulse picked up every time she saw him around town.

She jerked herself back to the real world. "You're the first person to ask me that. Most people just assume since he's a runaway he must be a punk."

He shrugged. "And sometimes it's not the kid who needs a good kick in the ass."

Sara agreed, knowing runaway cases weren't always as simple as a kid acting out against parents. Still, she hadn't found any evidence contrary to David's father's assertion that that's exactly what his son was doing. She couldn't exactly say she liked the guy, but no evidence was no evidence.

"Even so, he doesn't need to be out on his own. It's too dangerous."

"Could be." Adam's gaze met hers. "But a boy that age can take care of himself better than a lot of people think he can."

Sara wondered why he'd say such a thing, but it wasn't her business or relevant to her investigation. She took two more cards from her pocket and gave them to Adam and Suz.

"Nevertheless, I'd like a call if you hear or see anything that might help me find him."

Even though Adam nodded and slipped the card into his shorts pocket, she wasn't entirely convinced he would call her. She bit the inside of her jaw to remind herself she was being stupid to want to talk to him again, about anything.

A scream pierced the air behind Sara. She spun and scanned the beach for the source. A clump of people stood at the edge of the pier looking down at the water.

Adam cursed behind her. "A kid just went over the side."

Sara kicked off her shoes and unstrapped her gun at the same time. When she plopped it atop the bar, Adam was already running toward the side of the building. She met Suz's eyes. "Keep this."

She raced after Adam, who was almost halfway to the pier. The concession shed where he normally worked was a blur as she ran past it. Adam didn't pause as he reached the end of the pier and catapulted over the railing into the water below. She yelled for the bystanders to get out of the way before she followed him.

The water closed over her head, murkier than it looked from the pier. She glanced around before pushing up to the surface to fill her lungs. Adam popped up near her and searched the area around him.

"See him?" she asked.

"No." And then he dived under again. She wasn't about to let a kid drown so she did the same.

She held her breath and spotted the child just as Adam wrapped his arms around the little boy. Sara followed them to the surface then swam alongside

Adam toward the shore. As soon as they hit sand, she started CPR. The hysterical crying of some woman, probably the child's mother, barely filtered through the thundering of Sara's pulse against her eardrums.

After a couple of repetitions of CPR, the child coughed and began spitting up the water he'd swallowed. Sara helped him sit up. His mother swooped in and clasped him to her as Sara heard someone say an ambulance had been called.

She sat back and pushed the wet strands of her hair back from her forehead. Her heart had just begun to slow when she spotted Adam across from her. Rivulets of water ran down his bare chest, lightly sprinkled with hair, causing her heart rate to accelerate again. She'd seen him pull his shirt over his head and toss it onto the sand as they'd raced for the pier.

Now, with the danger over, her attention was drawn to what the shirt had hidden.

Good grief, what was wrong with her? Postadrenaline craziness? She forced herself to shift her gaze up to his face and noticed he looked pale, shaken.

"Are you okay?" she asked.

He kept staring at the kid for a couple more seconds then seemed to shake himself out of a trance. "Yeah, fine." He refocused on her—first her face, then lower. That's when she realized that her shirt was sticking to her like a second skin, the wet, white fabric revealing her bra underneath.

She didn't totally believe his assertion that he was fine, but she let it drop. After all, it wasn't every day you almost witnessed someone die.

"You did a good job," she said.

"You, too."

They sat on the sand until they heard the ambulance siren arrive in the parking lot beyond the dunes. Then Sara helped the mother and crying child stand. Once the paramedics had ushered the pair to the ambulance, Sara and Adam had to face all the questions posed by the police officer who'd responded. Then those of the reporter from the local paper who'd arrived about two seconds later. Adam looked as if he'd rather skydive with a parachute made of lead, and all Sara wanted to do was go home and take a shower in water that didn't smell like fish.

"Sure you don't want that drink?" Adam asked.

"Alas, still on duty."

Plus, she doubted Adam Canfield was on the drink menu.

ADAM TOOK a long drink of lemonade, wishing it was something stronger, as he watched Detective Sara Greene walk toward the dunes. She'd strapped her sidearm back on, the only thing she wore that wasn't dripping wet. Why did women go into dangerous professions like law enforcement? Why did they deliberately put themselves in the line of fire? Why couldn't they understand that it was useless to be a do-gooder out to solve the world's ills when the world had too many ills to solve?

He shook his head. Not his problem. Sure, she was pretty and built very nicely if the wet shirt had been any indication, but there were way too many babes walking the sands of Horizon Beach for him to even think about pursuing a woman who was his complete opposite. He didn't need to have a Ph.D. to know she didn't think highly of the code he lived by—to be as carefree as possible and screw responsibility.

Heck, even helping out at the bar where he was normally a patron was a stretch. But Zac, his best friend here in his adopted hometown, had asked him to lend a hand while he and his new wife, Randi, were on their honeymoon. He couldn't wait for them to come home so he could go back to his regular job—running the pier concession just enough to pay his bills.

Even after Sara disappeared from view, he couldn't get the sight of her dark hair and eyes out of his head. Suz Thackery, who was the head cheese at the Beach Bum in Zac's absence, nudged him out of the way.

"Stop drooling on yourself. It's bad for business."

He jerked his gaze away from the crossover point on the dunes and tossed a towel at Suz. "I wasn't drooling. Just wondering about that missing kid."

"Uh-huh." Suz gave him a disbelieving look. "I give it less than twenty-four hours before you make up some excuse to call her."

He shook his head. "She's way too serious for me." But he knew if Sara Greene were a secretary or mail carrier or worked in an ice cream parlor, he might look at her differently.

Suz moved to the opposite end of the bar to refill the older couple's lemonades and open three beers for some college-age guys who'd come in from boogie boarding. Adam dug around in the storage room until he found the extra clothes Zac kept in the back in case he got alcohol spilled on him during a shift. He exchanged his wet shorts for a dry pair, but no way was he wearing a pair of his friend's underwear.

When a delivery arrived, he spent several minutes lugging crates of beer and stacking them in the storeroom. After placing the last case in cold storage, he sank onto it to cool off. As soon as he sat, he imagined bringing Sara Greene back here to this cool, dark spot and kissing her.

He ran his hand over his hair and cursed. He must have hit his head on the pier. Plenty of women were interested in him without him daydreaming about one who wasn't. He didn't go looking for brainless women, just ones who were casual and laid-back. He'd deliberately kept things easy and noncommittal with women since he'd moved to Horizon Beach. After serving a dozen years in the army and being shipped to one hot, sandy, inhospitable place after another, he deserved a carefree life. One filled with the ocean, fishing the days away and bikini-clad babes as far as the eye could see.

Nothing that would require him to think or remember. Or care for someone.

He shot to his feet and resisted the urge to punch one of the cases of liquor surrounding him. The nightmare was only supposed to attack him when he was sleeping, when his guard was down. But the memory of the Humvee shooting toward the sky was burned into his gray matter.

He reminded himself once again that a do-gooder like Sara was off-limits. He'd been down that bomb-riddled road before and had almost not lived to tell about it.

Sometimes he wished he hadn't.

THE AFTEREFFECTS of the near drowning plus the frustration at not finding any clues to David Taylor's whereabouts occupied so much of Sara's mind that she forgot to stop at the Coffee Cottage on the way back to the station after going home to change. Faced with having to drink the barely liquid coffee Keith Hutchens had made, she detoured toward the soda machine and bought a can of caffeine-laden Coke instead.

As she entered the bull-pen area of the station, she passed Keith just as he was headed out on patrol. "There's still coffee." He nodded toward the break room.

"Keith, I hate to break it to you, but I'm pretty sure what's in that coffeepot is used motor oil."

"Nobody around here appreciates a good black coffee."

Sara laughed as Keith walked toward the back door.

By the time she reached her desk, however, the laugh had died away. She examined the photo of David Taylor again. He was a cute kid with dark hair and light eyes—blue, based on his father's description. Though he was smiling in the picture of him standing by his school locker, there was something about him that seemed a little off, maybe even sad.

The question Adam Canfield had asked replayed in her head. "What *is* he running from?" she murmured.

No matter how long she stared at the picture, the answer didn't reveal itself. Nor did his whereabouts. She hated the idea of him out there alone.

"Heard we nearly had a tragedy at the pier earlier."

She tossed the picture onto her desk and looked up at her boss, Captain Mark Pierce.

"Yeah. But everything turned out okay."

Pierce pointed at the photo. "Any luck?"

"Nothing since we got the call from the lady who said she thought she saw him on the edge of town."

The captain shook his head. "No telling where he is. Could be hundreds of miles in any direction."

Sara's heart squeezed at the thought. She wasn't ready to believe he was beyond her help yet. "He's young and has limited funds. I don't think he's gotten very far. That's just a gut feeling though."

"Well, I've been at this long enough to respect a gut feeling." Pierce rapped his knuckles against the edge of her desk. "Keep working it, but don't let the other stuff go."

She nodded before he turned to walk away, leaving her to heave a sigh and look at the pile of work on her desk. How did detectives in larger cities handle it? Horizon Beach was far from a metropolis or a hotbed of crime, and still she stayed busy from the moment she came on shift until the moment she left. And sometimes beyond that.

The picture of David went back into the manila folder that held all the information about the case, though that was precious little. With only a few minutes left on her shift, she decided to tackle the pile of mail and pulled out a letter opener. Among the items that went directly into the trash and those that she deposited in various case files, she found two tickets to the Helping Hands Ball, the annual dance and auction to benefit special programs hosted by the police and fire departments.

She sighed as she stared at them. It seemed as if she'd attended the ball only weeks ago instead of months. And she was no closer to finding the right man now than she'd been then.

The image of Adam Canfield popped into her head, making her snort at the very idea of him in that role. She shoved the tickets back into their envelope and then into her desk drawer. That she was even thinking about him again annoyed her. Her common sense rebelled at the idea that she found him attractive, that it had taken all her willpower not to turn around to see if he was watching her as she'd left the Beach Bum earlier.

Of course he hadn't been. She wasn't the kind of woman Adam made the effort to watch.

She pushed the unwanted thoughts away and glanced at the framed photo of her daughters sitting on the corner of her desk, huge smiles stretching across their faces. Her number-one priority remained being the best mother she could be to Lilly and Tana and finding them a good, solid father who could love them, dote on them, as her father had loved her.

"Isn't your shift over?"

Sara jerked out of her thoughts and looked up at Captain Pierce where he'd stopped on his way out.

"Um, yeah. Just cleaning up a bit of mail before I leave." And trying not to fantasize about what Adam Canfield looked like with water glistening on his naked chest.

Captain Pierce left, but Sara still took a couple of minutes to get her brain back in correct working order. She used the ten-minute drive home to get into mommy mode and leave inappropriate daydreams behind.

After parking her car in front of her little yellow

bungalow, she crossed the street to the home of Ruby Phelps, the girls' babysitter. As soon as she stepped inside the door, three-year-old Lilly squealed, "Mommy!" and ran over to give Sara a hug and a big, sloppy kiss. Sara never got tired of hearing her adopted girls say that.

"How's my little peanut?" Sara asked as she hugged her daughter back.

"Nummy."

"She just had an oatmeal raisin cookie. Come in and have one." Ruby stood wiping her hands on a towel in the doorway to the kitchen.

"Sounds good. I'm running on fumes." Sara was suddenly glad it was Friday afternoon and she was looking at two days off to spend with the girls.

Ruby motioned her into the kitchen. "I made plenty, so help yourself."

Sara followed the older woman into the cheery kitchen and snagged a fresh cookie from the plate in the middle of the table. Tana sat at one end of the table with a cookie in one hand and a pen put to notebook in the other. Sara looked at her thirteen-year-old with affection. Tana's adoption paperwork had yet to be finalized, but Sara already thought of the three of them as a family.

"Hey, how was school?"

"Good. I have a project to do for science this weekend, but I need to go to the pier to do it."

Sara cringed inside. The memory of nearly losing

that little boy today caused her to abandon the cookie.

"Can't you go somewhere else?"

"Nope."

Sara sighed. The last place she wanted to go on her day off was the pier where Adam Canfield ran the concession, taking the money of locals and tourists who wanted to fish or walk on the pier that jutted into the Gulf of Mexico. The pier that happened to be next to the Beach Bum, his home away from home. The pier where she'd had wildly inappropriate thoughts about him. If she hadn't believed in fate having a wicked sense of humor before, she did now.

"What kind of project?"

Tana looked up, her dark eyes serious. "I have to spend an hour at the pier and list all the types of fish reeled in by the fishermen. Then I have to research the details about their populations and migration patterns."

"Seventh grade sure has changed a lot since I was there," Sara said.

"Well, yeah. That was ages ago."

Sara tossed a cookie crumb at Tana. "It wasn't *that* long ago, smarty-pants."

Tana just smiled and took another large bite of her cookie.

"We'll go in the morning, before it gets too hot." Might as well get it over with. Maybe Adam would be too sleepy or hungover to even know she was there.

After a couple minutes of chitchat with Ruby, Sara ushered the girls across the street to their own house. She wanted nothing more than to shuck her slacks, dress flats and button-up shirt and sink into a warm bath. Well, perhaps there was something she wanted more than that, but realistic expectations topped out with a foamy, hot, scented bath. First she had to make dinner and spend some quality time with the girls.

A knock on the door turned out to be Ruby. She held out Lilly's favorite Winnie-the-Pooh blanket as she stepped inside the front door. "I knew you wouldn't be able to get her to sleep tonight without it."

"Thanks."

Ruby tilted her head slightly. "You okay? You seem like you have something on your mind."

"Just a long day."

Ruby made sure the girls weren't close by. "I heard about what happened at the pier. That little boy okay?"

"Yeah." Thanks to Adam. He might not be the guy for her, but he'd saved a child's life today. "But I spent most of the day looking for a fourteen-year-old runaway who seems to have disappeared into thin air. I looked for that boy everywhere, and no one's seen him."

"People who don't want to be found have a way of staying hidden. Wonder what he's running from."

Sara examined the other woman's lightly lined

face as Ruby pushed her chin-length silver hair behind her ear. "You're the second person to say something like that today."

"Who was the other?"

Sara waved off the question. "Nobody important. Main thing is that I couldn't find the kid, and at best he's spending tonight out there alone somewhere."

"Sweetie, you can only do so much."

Sara heaved a sigh. "I know."

Ruby patted her arm. "You need to plan a day off just for yourself, maybe do something crazy like go on an actual date."

"I go on dates."

Ruby crossed her arms and gave Sara a hairy-eyeball look from behind her rimless glasses. "When was the last one?"

Sara opened her mouth to answer but then realized she didn't know what to say.

Ruby tapped her forefinger against Sara's hand. "My point exactly."

"Horizon Beach doesn't exactly have a huge dating pool."

"Maybe your parameters are too strict," Ruby said with a twinkle in her eye. "Loosen up a bit. It's dating, not lifetime commitment."

As Ruby turned to leave, Sara bit down on a reply that she knew what she wanted, so why should she waste time with guys who didn't fit the bill?

And Adam Canfield so didn't fit the bill.

Chapter Two

Adam's street was quiet and dark when he rolled in to his driveway after work. Of course, it would be at nearly two in the morning. The only sounds that met his ears when he stepped out of the car were the distant waves and the hum of air conditioners.

This wasn't the first time he'd arrived home at this hour, but being on the opposite side of the bar added a great deal to his fatigue level. Not to mention way too many questions from patrons when they'd found out he was the one who'd dived off the pier after that kid. How many days until Zac came back?

Okay, he needed to suck it up and just deal because Zac and Randi deserved a nice, long honeymoon after everything they'd been through. Arson, false accusations, damn near getting killed.

Sure, it was odd having his best friend be a married man now, but damned if he wasn't happy for him. He guessed it would be nice to know you could go home to someone who loved you every night, sleep in late tangled in the same sheets.

That image pulled Sara Greene back into his thoughts. Ugh. He needed to get some sleep, not get worked up about a woman he'd already decided not to pursue. He rubbed his hand over his face and headed toward his front door. But a noise from the side of the house caused him to stop and listen. When he heard it again, he edged along the front until he reached the corner.

Movement at the back of his property caught his eye. It looked like someone hurrying from his backyard into that of his neighbor on the next street. He crossed the lawn to the point where he'd seen the shape, scanned his neighbor's property, but saw nothing. Considering he was way too tired to give chase even if he did see someone, he retraced his steps to the house.

His doors were locked, but he still searched the house to make sure no one was inside or that anything was missing. After a few minutes, he was satisfied whoever had been out there hadn't broken in. Good, because he was too exhausted to deal with cops and police reports for the second time in a day. He just wanted to fall into bed and sleep for twelve hours. Too bad he only had five.

He pitched his sweaty T-shirt into the laundry basket in the corner, but when he started to take off his shorts he remembered the business card in his pocket. He pulled it out and sank onto the side of the bed. Sara Greene's phone number taunted him, seeming to pulse an invitation to call it.

For a moment, he considered his prowler might have been young David Taylor. Then he would have a legitimate reason to call Sara. But with nothing to support his wild theory, he tossed the card onto his nightstand and flopped back on the bed, his feet still on the floor.

Why was his brain refusing to let go of her image? Sure, she had dark, shiny hair, dark eyes and nice curves, but he'd seen her several times before and not reacted this way.

Had to be fatigue. Or some crazy nonsense like the lure of the unavailable.

Or the fact she'd leapt off the pier after him to save a child. He might want to steer clear of women who put themselves in danger, but it evidently didn't mean he couldn't be wildly attracted to one in the aftermath of that danger.

As his eyes drifted shut, he imagined what it'd be like to run his hands through her hair and kiss her lips. That image accompanied him as his consciousness gradually gave way to sleep. The feel of her silky hair, the wetness of her kiss, some flowery smell that seemed to cling to attractive women, the softness of her skin moving against his.

It felt so good. His body flamed in response as he wrapped his arms around her. Shielding her from whatever was lurking out there in the dark. Because something was lurking, trying to steal the joy enveloping his heart.

Images flew at him, each one more frightening. Each one causing him to wrap more fully around Sara, protecting her. No, not Sara. But it wasn't enough, he thought a moment before the explosion, before the pain.

Adam jerked awake, shaking and sweating and his leg on fire from the pain.

Remembered pain.

He shoved himself to a sitting position and stared at the scar lining his thigh, a forever reminder of that day that refused to die in his memory.

Damn it. He dropped his head into his upturned palms and pressed against his eyeballs in a vain effort to make the images go away. He'd been having such a nice dream. Why the hell had it insisted on flowing into the nightmare that haunted him like a curse?

Because maybe he needed the reminder to stay away from women like Sara Greene, no matter how nice the daydreams about her were.

Tomorrow he needed to find a simple, carefree date, someone to make him forget about Sara Greene and his inexplicable reaction to her.

He sighed and ran his fingers back through his rumpled hair. And tried to ignore a little voice that whispered doing so wouldn't be as easy as it should be.

LILLY SQUEALED in delight as she ran through the sand on the beach. Sara smiled and her heart expanded as she watched her daughter enjoy every moment of life and its many exciting sights and sounds. Lilly was a little bubble of sunshine and joy who had no idea her life had started out so sadly, that her birth mother had abandoned her at the hospital when she was only a couple of days old.

"Oh, big bird!" she said as she pointed toward a pelican diving toward the surf.

"It should be against the law to be that chipper this early in the morning," Tana said as she trudged along beside Sara. "I demand you arrest her."

Sara laughed and wrapped her arm around Tana's shoulders. "What's not to like? It's beautiful, the breeze is nice and cool, the beach isn't crowded yet."

"That's because normal people are still asleep."

Sara ruffled Tana's short chestnut hair. "It's not like I got you up at the crack of dawn."

Tana's guttural response made it clear she didn't like the hour, no matter its proximity to the break of day.

As they approached the pier, Sara scooped up Lilly so she wouldn't lose her off the edge or in the throng of early-morning anglers. The idea of Lilly falling into that murky water chilled Sara all the way through. She pulled money from her shorts pocket to pay the pier walking fee and prepared herself to face Adam again. When she stepped up in front of the concession stand, Adam stared back at her from sleep-heavy eyes. She stifled her laughter.

"Hours not agreeing with you?" she asked, fighting a smile.

"Can you get early mornings outlawed?"

"Seems to be a popular idea. I'll get right on that."

Sara glanced around the interior of the small shack, at the small TV muted on ESPN, at the stack of magazines on the table next to a tall stool, the casual shirt and cargo shorts Adam was wearing. He definitely looked like a beach bum, but the best-looking one she'd seen in years. That thought erased her mirth.

Why couldn't Tana's science project have required them to go to the Gulfarium or something?

"At least this is an even less taxing job than standing behind a bar," she said.

"Just the way I like it, nice and easy."

Not a lot of ambition in that statement, but that wasn't news.

She lowered her gaze and thought of Ruby's words from the day before. The way her senses were sparking, she did need to find a date soon. But if she was going to spend even more time away from home and the girls, she had to find a more likely candidate. Someone who might turn into something more for her, Tana and Lilly. The idea of Adam Canfield as a family man was laughable to the point of being ludicrous.

"So, I'm guessing from the lack of rods and

tackle boxes that you all are just walking the pier this morning?"

Sara nodded as she handed over the pier walking fees. "Tana has a school project to work on here."

"Hmm," he said as he put the cash in the register. "Can't remember any homework that allowed me to be outside on a pretty day."

Sara sensed the "old" comment was on the tip of Tana's tongue, so she spoke first. "Evidently we're ancient and school has changed a lot since cavemen were grunting at each other."

Tana snickered. Sara pushed her playfully on the shoulder.

Adam leaned forward on the counter lining the front of the small building. Sara's eyes went straight to his tanned, sinewy arms and imagined them pulling her to him. Oh, good grief, she shouldn't be having those kinds of thoughts with the girls right next to her. But how was she supposed to not have them when he stood there looking like the cosmos's gift to sex-starved women?

He nodded to both girls and met Tana's gaze. "So, what kind of homework does one do at a fishing pier?"

Sara couldn't help watching Adam as Tana explained her assignment and he pointed out the best fishermen to ask her questions. He actually paid attention to Tana, talked to her as if she was an adult. Something about that surprised Sara, wormed its way past the negative view she had of Adam.

Lilly squirmed in her arms. "Down."

Sara smiled at her little pixie as she lowered Lilly to her pink-sandaled feet. Lilly didn't like to be confined. Trying to harness her almost constant motion for very long was a bit like corraling a tornado. But Sara refused to let go of her hand.

Considering she didn't know what else to say to Adam or how she felt about what had just transpired, Sara ushered the girls toward the end of the pier where fishermen were already reeling in redfish, pompano and ladyfish. Tana jumped right in asking the lucky anglers about their catches, especially the ones Adam had pointed out. She looked like a miniature reporter with her pen and spiral-bound notebook.

Lilly soaked up all the activity around her, but Sara didn't allow her to venture farther than a couple of steps from where Sara sat on a bench enjoying the salty, warm air. Sometimes it seemed as if she'd lived here forever instead of only three years. The two times she'd gone back to Memphis, she'd felt trapped without the sea air and the sound of the waves. Odd since she'd spent the first twenty-five years of her life in the home of Elvis, blues and the mighty, muddy Mississippi River. But she'd fallen irrevocably in love with Horizon Beach's stretches of sugar-white sand overlooking blue-green water.

She loved her home, her job, her girls. Only one thing was missing. If she stopped looking for the right guy, would he walk into her life?

Momentary weakness made her look toward the building on the other end of the pier. No Adam in sight. She didn't know if she was glad or disheartened by his absence.

She redirected her gaze to a ship on the distant horizon, likely a navy vessel headed toward Pensacola. An unbidden wave of loneliness hit her. Her watch showed she had to sit where she was for another forty-seven minutes. How had only thirteen minutes of the hour Tana was required to stay at the pier passed? She glanced in Adam's direction again and saw him talking to a family loaded down with fishing gear.

This morning sure would be easier to endure if Adam Canfield were three shades of ugly.

But he wasn't. Far from it.

She pulled her gaze away from the concession hut and back toward the people lining the pier. Most were men. Perhaps one of them was the type of date she sought.

Some she scratched from the list because she simply wasn't attracted. Others wore wedding bands or showed evidence of habits she didn't like and refused to have her daughters exposed to. That left only a couple remotely attractive candidates, but she had no idea how to actually meet them.

Maybe it was time to give online dating a try. A disgusted sound escaped her as she considered the possibility.

"That bored, huh?"

Adam's voice was as sexy as the rest of him. Her torment was complete.

She pointed toward the long line of fishermen. "Not really my thing."

"You ever tried it?"

"Not in the ocean. But I went with my dad on the river, a couple of lakes."

"Not the same. The fish here give you more of a challenge, a bigger workout to reel them in."

"Last thing I want to do on my day off is fight with something."

He stared at her for a beat before saying, "Right."

Any hint of his fun-loving self disappeared, and Sara mourned its loss. Now he was all business as he shoved his hands in his pockets. "It might be nothing, but I had a prowler at my place last night."

"Patrol typically works thefts."

"Nothing was taken. House wasn't even broken into. But I saw someone running out of my backyard, and for some reason I thought of the kid you were looking for. He still missing?"

Lilly bumped into her knee, and without looking Sara pulled her daughter up onto her lap, held her close as if talking about one missing child would make her own disappear.

"Yes. Did you get a look at the person? How big was he?"

Adam shook his head. "I couldn't see him well, couldn't even swear it was a him. Didn't follow whoever it was. Too dead on my feet. I doubt I could have caught a turtle at that point."

"Plus, not a good idea to chase unknown prowlers into the night."

"True," he said. "I looked around the backyard this morning but didn't find anything."

"I'd still like to take a look."

"Be my guest." He said it as though he didn't expect her to find anything, either, and he might be right.

Still, she had to search for herself. When her brain had been fixating on him and her hormones, she should have been trying to figure out where else to look for David Taylor.

"Sometime later today?" This was a serious matter, and yet a sizzle passed through her when her eyes met his.

He didn't say anything for a few seconds. When he finally broke eye contact, he shifted his weight from one foot to the other. "Sure. I don't get off work until one, but you can go by without me there. It's 715 Conch."

She nodded.

"Well, see ya later."

At his goodbye, Lilly gave him a big smile and an enthusiastic wave. "Bye-bye."

He looked startled by Lilly's gestures, but he gave her a half smile and a little wave back. He couldn't have looked more uncomfortable if he'd tried.

Chapter Three

Sara took deep, slow, quiet breaths as she drove down Conch Avenue. This was a potential lead in an investigation, nothing more. If she were lucky, she'd find some clue Adam had overlooked. It'd bring her closer to finding David Taylor and occupy her mind with work instead of images of Adam that refused to go away.

Not since she'd had a major crush on Steve Dane in the ninth grade had she felt this type of all-consuming yearning for someone. Only this was more powerful, more adult than her feelings for Steve had ever been. And if she were being honest, that scared her. She had a life plan, and tall, sexy and not particularly driven wasn't a part of it. Though she had to admit she wondered if there was some hidden side to Adam, something other than physical attraction that was pulling her toward him. He'd already proven himself a hero. He and his actions at the pier were on the front page of the paper for all to see.

What was she thinking? She'd seen him with more women than she could count. She didn't want to become one of the many former dates of Adam Canfield.

"This is cool," Tana said from the passenger seat. "Going out on a real case."

"You and Lilly will stay by the car."

"Ah, come on. I want to see what you do."

"This isn't that exciting," Sara said as she eyed house numbers. "I'm just going to be walking around a backyard seeing if someone dropped anything identifiable."

Which was a stretch.

"I can help look."

"No."

"Why not?"

Sara glanced at Tana, at her eager face. She'd been curious about Sara's job ever since she'd brought her home two years ago. "Because you're not trained to know what to look for, and I'm pretty sure the department would frown on me bringing two kids to work with me."

"But you're not on the clock today. We could all just be visiting a friend."

"Well, that wouldn't exactly be true, would it?"

"Adam could be a friend."

Sara rolled her eyes at Tana's persistence and went back to checking addresses. When she spotted 715, she wasn't surprised to find it was a totally unadorned bachelor residence. While his next-door neighbor displayed several hanging pots of bright purple and pink bougainvillea, his little white clapboard house sported an unremarkable lawn, a few untrimmed bushes along the front of the house and a leaning mailbox.

She pulled in to the driveway. "Remember, stay close to the car and watch your sister."

"Fine." Tana didn't sound as if she thought it was fine, but she really was a good kid and Sara could depend on her to make sure Lilly didn't do something like wander into the street. The two of them weren't biological siblings, not even adopted sisters yet, but Sara had treated them like sisters from the moment they both came to live with her.

Sara reached over and ruffled Tana's hair a little. "I'll try to be quick. Then we'll go get something to eat."

Tana swatted Sara's hand away like a normal annoyed teenager. Sara smiled as she got out of the car.

She reined in that smile, however, when she spotted Adam stepping out of the side door into the carport where his little black sports car sat. If she started smiling at him, she might not be able to stop.

She mentally kicked herself for not making it here earlier, before he got home. But she hadn't expected him here so soon. It was barely after one o'clock.

Sara steeled herself, focused on the fact that right now she was a detective working a case, not a woman appreciating a man's very fine physical attributes.

Adam nodded to the girls as she approached him.

"I see you brought backup. Little early to have them in training, isn't it?"

He said it with a hint of humor, but she still felt like she'd made a bad parenting decision bringing them. Not that she'd had much of a choice. Ruby was visiting her sister in Panama City, and time was of the essence when working a missing child case.

"Their sitter is out of town today." She took a few more steps to look into his backyard. "Tell me exactly what you heard and saw."

He repeated the story of how he'd come home late after the bar closed, had heard something around the side of his house, had eased to the corner to check it out and seen someone disappearing into the neighbor's yard.

Sara searched the carport, examined the windows and door lining the back of Adam's house for signs of attempted entry. After checking the entire backyard, particularly the spot where he'd seen the person leave the area, she sighed in defeat.

"See, nada," he said as he leaned against an old metal clothesline pole.

She scanned the yard one more time, frustrated that the person hadn't left behind any clue to his or her identity. "Could have been anyone. David, someone casing the neighborhood for theft purposes, a teenager taking a shortcut home."

When she glanced at Adam, he was watching her with a question in his eyes. "What?"

"Just curious."

"About?"

"When I first met you, I didn't peg you for a cop. But when you slip into work mode, it's obvious."

"I'm not sure you mean that as a good or bad thing."

"Both."

"Care to elaborate?" As if she could concentrate with his white T-shirt doing nice, sculpting things for his upper body.

"It's good that you're looking for this kid."

"Thought you said he could take care of himself."

"Maybe he can, maybe not."

She shifted her weight and lifted her hand to shade her eyes from the sun. "And the bad part of me being a cop?"

"Not sure I want to reveal that to someone who packs a gun." He grinned, making it obvious how all those women had ended up on his arm.

"You don't believe in women being police officers?"

He shook his head. "I'm not taking that bait. Just seems a dangerous career choice for anyone."

"Living is dangerous."

The muscles in his face tightened, and a darkness seemed to settle on him. "Can't argue with that."

He pushed away from the pole and headed back toward the driveway. She followed, wondering what had prompted him to comment on her choice of career. Chalk up his disagreement with that choice as another reason to steer clear of him until her little infatuation faded away.

He nodded toward the girls. "When I first saw you with them, I thought you were babysitting. But someone told me they're yours."

Sara squinted at him and the abrupt change of subject before responding.

"Yeah. They were in foster care."

"You adopted them?"

"Yes."

"You must stay really busy."

"I do, but I'm never bored."

He laughed a little, and she liked the sound of it, deep and rich.

As they approached her car, Tana gave her a funny look she couldn't read. It looked…mischievous somehow, but Sara couldn't imagine what she might be up to. Had Tana wandered away from the car when she wasn't looking?

Lilly tugged on Tana's hand as if trying to get her into the car.

"She's getting hungry," Tana said as she resisted her little sister's efforts.

Lilly stopped tugging on the immovable Tana. "Pizza!" she said as she jumped up and down and clapped her hands.

Adam laughed as he stepped up beside Sara. "Guess we know what she wants."

"We're going to Freddie's," Tana said. "You should tag along so you and Sara can talk more."

Sara's eyes widened as she heard the words come out of Tana's mouth. "Mr. Canfield and I are done here." She looked at Adam briefly, doing her best to suppress a blush. "If you hear or see anything else, let me know."

"Will do." He looked at her funny, too, as if he knew what was going on in her flustered brain and found it amusing.

Once she and the girls were in the car, with both girls waving to Adam, Sara resisted the urge to flee from the street at a high rate of speed.

"What was that all about?" she asked Tana.

"He's hot. You should go out with him."

Sara's mouth dropped open, but she couldn't speak until they reached the end of the street. "Just because someone is 'hot' doesn't mean you automatically go out with him." Geez, the guy had charmed a barely teen and a three-year-old without even trying.

"So you *do* think he's good-looking."

Sara rolled her eyes. "You've been listening to Ruby too much."

"You've always said Ruby's a smart lady."

Trapped by her own words. Sara resisted the need to bang her head against the steering wheel.

ADAM WAVED AT THE GIRLS, still confused by how friendly they were toward him but amused by it, as

well, since it flustered Sara. She seemed too serious
and in need of a good fluster.

His mouth watered, but he fought the sudden
desire for Freddie's pizza. After all, it was the best
pizza in town.

Instead, he went back inside and stared into his refrigerator. When a half-eaten pack of lunch meat and
a leftover taco stared back at him, he acknowledged
the cruel fact that he'd have to go grocery shopping
soon.

But not today. He downed a few corn chips and
decided he needed some more sleep if he was going
to get through another night at the bar.

He noticed that morning's paper with his image
plastered on the front page. He ground his teeth as
he read the headline again—the one proclaiming
him a hero. He was anything but a hero. On his way
to the bedroom, he pitched the paper in the trash can
with enough force that it rocked before settling back
into its spot.

Dreams invaded his sleep again, but this time no
one was killed. No one was in the desert of Iraq. And
the woman in his dream made him feel very, very
good.

When Adam woke, the need for a long, cold
shower soaked into his brain. It flowed past all the
lingering images and feelings from the dream of him
and Sara getting to know each other in something
other than a professional capacity. He closed his eyes

and relived the dream until the fact that she wasn't real and warm and soft in his arms right that minute caused him to growl and head toward the shower.

Was he doomed to never have a decent night's sleep again? If nightmares weren't ripping at him, dreams about enthusiastic sex with a woman he'd sworn to avoid had his body buzzing.

He stripped and stepped into the shower. Tonight, he was going to be at his flirting best, and maybe he'd hook up with someone who'd make thoughts of Sara Greene fade away for good.

It didn't work. That night or the next or the…hell, nearly a week went by without relief. No matter how much he tried to work up interest in the women he met across the bar, he couldn't. His fixation on Sara made no sense.

"Little off your game, aren't you?" Suz asked at one point.

"Bite me."

Suz laughed and went to mix a couple of drinks for the Friday evening crowd.

As if things weren't turned upside down enough, he looked across the bar and spotted Sara step into the Beach Bum with several guys. He recognized them as local cops, probably out for a drink after work. She glanced in his direction and caught his gaze for a moment before returning her attention to her friends.

Adam fisted his hands and redoubled his efforts

in flirting with Candy, a stunning blonde who'd parked herself at the bar. But his eyes kept veering toward Sara.

SARA HAD DONE PRETTY well all week, filling her days with work and activities with the girls to keep her mind off the man she couldn't have, shouldn't want. Each time she started to fantasize about Adam, she reminded herself that she deserved more than a love-'em-and-leave-'em kind of guy. The girls deserved people in their lives who wouldn't end up leaving.

Work had kept her extra busy. In addition to the David Taylor case, a couple more had come across her desk. It'd been one of those weeks when she'd eaten fast food on the run for too many meals and one day ran into the next.

By the time another Friday afternoon had arrived, she'd spent the last few minutes of her shift staring at the top of her messy desk. And wondering what had happened to the world when even a small town like Horizon Beach had enough cases to keep two detectives and a dozen patrolmen busy.

When some of the guys had invited her out for a wind-down drink after work, she'd uncharacteristically said yes. She really did need the down time before going home. After all, in addition to Ruby's persistent assertion that Sara needed time for herself, Tana had told Sara that morning that she "needed a life." She hadn't said it in a mean way, more matter of fact, which was Tana's usual way of approaching any and all things. She said what she thought without beating around the bush.

But Sara wanted to draw the line on "getting a life" at hanging out at the Beach Bum, which is where Keith had chosen for the after-work drinks. She nearly backed out when she followed Keith into the parking lot and realized his destination, but she'd never been that big of a chicken.

Instead, she followed Keith, Shawn Winters and her fellow detective, Peter Jensen, to the open table at the front edge of the bar. At least it was as far away from Adam as she could get and still be in the Beach Bum. Despite telling herself not to, she glanced toward the bar and wished she hadn't.

Adam was leaning in close toward a stunningly beautiful woman. From their laughter and a wink she saw Adam shoot the woman's way, it was obvious he was on his way to his latest conquest.

Well, good.

Not good.

Dang it, she couldn't decide. What was it about him that made her veer toward crazy? And why now, when she'd known who he was for months? Because she kept crossing paths with him now? Because she'd been alone for so long? Because she'd seen him shirtless and being all heroic?

A waitress brought beers for the guys and a rum

and Coke for Sara. She sucked half of it down too fast and choked.

"You okay?" Keith gave her a funny look.

She nodded. "Yeah. Just thirsty." And fighting the urge to find some reason to arrest the blonde at the bar.

Sara tried to follow the conversations about football, the new barbecue place in town and the patrolman who'd been arrested in Pensacola for soliciting a prostitute—really she did. But her attention kept getting diverted to Adam and the woman, whose laughter managed to carry over all the noise in the bar.

"Greene, why do you keep staring at the bartender?" Shawn asked her. "You like him or something?"

She didn't like the sound of the teasing, not when she'd worked hard to fit into what was still very much a man's world. So she gave it back. "How could I like anyone else when my heart belongs to you?" She batted her eyelashes for extra dramatic effect.

Peter and Keith howled, and Peter slapped Shawn on the back. Shawn picked a peanut out of the bowl in the middle of the table and flipped it at her. She dodged it and laughed. This outing would be good and relaxing if not for her hyperawareness of Adam. Before she slipped up and glanced at him again, she decided to give Shawn what sounded like a real answer.

"He was one of the people I talked to about David Taylor. He had a prowler at his house, and he thought it could have been David."

"What made him think that?" Peter asked.

"Just a wild guess. I went out there and looked around but didn't find anything."

Shawn still looked at her as if he knew she was hiding something. Deciding that was her cue to leave, she nevertheless drank the rest of her rum and Coke more slowly than she had the first half. After downing the last of her drink and popping a few peanuts in her mouth, she tossed the necessary bills on the table.

"Well, you boys have a good night. I've got to pick up the girls."

And get the heck out of Adam Canfield's proximity.

As soon as she stood, however, loud shouts erupted in the middle of the crowd, followed by the sound of breaking glass and tumbled chairs.

"Great," Keith mumbled. "Can't even have a drink in peace."

The fight between several large men went from bad to worse in like a second. Sara and her fellow officers jumped right into the thick of it, shoving and prying people apart. But as soon as they managed to separate the two combatants, others joined in.

Just fantastic.

Sara dodged a flying beer bottle a moment before it would have cracked against her forehead. She saw Keith get hold of a guy who looked as though he could be an NFL linebacker, but he lost his grip when the guy head-butted him. Her kingdom for a Taser.

Curses and alcohol flew through the air, and those not caught up in the melee fled out of the sides of the bar. Handy not having full walls in the way.

She spotted one of the instigators, who was smaller than the others, and reached for her handcuffs. But her hand slid off the metal when a punch came out of the craziness and hit her hard in the cheek. The power of the blow knocked her backward. She tumbled into other people on her way down to the floor.

Her brain rattled against her skull, and her vision blurred. On the verge of passing out, she couldn't garner enough power to pull herself out of the way of trampling feet.

But someone else did. One moment she was in danger of serious injury. The next, someone strong grabbed her under her arms and dragged her free and behind the safety of the polished-wood bar. Her vision cleared enough that when she looked up, she saw the face of her rescuer.

Adam Canfield, in all his green-eyed glory.

Chapter Four

Sara's breath caught in her chest for a moment as she stared up at Adam, who stared right back. Was it a sign of insanity to want to reach up and kiss him when there was chaos going on behind her? Probably.

Some iota of common sense clawed its way to the front of her mind and enabled her to break eye contact. She shifted so she could lift herself.

Adam gripped her arm, stopping her before she could stand. "Where do you think you're going?"

She gestured toward the fight. "To help out."

Adam nodded behind her. "I think your friends have it under control."

Sara turned and gritted her teeth against the searing pain that shot through her head. Shawn was handcuffing the last of the cursing combatants while Keith and Peter held the other two apart.

"You okay?" Keith asked when he spotted her position. "Saw you took a good wallop." By the way he handled the guy in his custody, she guessed Mr. Not-So-Happy was the one who'd punched her.

"I've had better days, but I'll live."

Keith looked past Sara to Adam. "Thanks, man."

"No problem. Glad you guys were here."

"You need to get checked out?" Shawn asked, his earlier teasing forgotten.

"Nah, I'm fine, really," she said, wishing the guys would stop fussing over her. "Just want to go home and spend some quality time with some ibuprofen."

"All right then," Shawn said. "We'll get these idiots outta here."

Sara sat on the floor, dreading moving, as she watched the guys shove the still-grumbling troublemakers out of the bar. Keith called for a couple of squad cars so they could dump the guys on some officers who were actually on the clock.

With a sigh, she shifted her feet and hands under her and pushed herself to a standing position. She blinked against the throb in her cheek. Damn, that was going to leave a mark. She was still riding out the pain as Adam guided her to a stool. Okay, she'd sit, just until her cheek stopped feeling like there was a fist embedded in it.

Adam stepped away, but only for a few seconds. He extended a plastic bag filled with ice. "Here. This will help to keep it from swelling so much."

Her hand brushed his as she took the ice pack. Despite her jaw feeling as if George Foreman had punched her, she jolted at the warm contact. She hesitated a little too long in bringing the ice to her cheek, so he guided her hand. She winced when the ice made contact with her skin and tried to pull it away, but Adam's hand gently held hers in place.

Instead of making the mistake of looking into his eyes again, she closed her own. "Guess I'm going to have a nice shiner in the morning."

"You ever think about getting a different job, one that's a little less dangerous?"

She opened her eyes and looked at him, tried to figure out why it even mattered to him what she did for a living. "Believe it or not, this isn't an everyday occurrence. I don't think there's going to be a *Law and Order: Horizon Beach* any time soon."

"Only takes once," he muttered as he moved away and started righting chairs while Suz swept up the glass.

Sara's natural inclination to dig until she found the answers to all her questions flared, but not enough to trump the pounding of her head and the supreme desire to go home. If this was what going out to have fun got her, she'd had enough, thanks.

"Well, thanks for the ice pack," she said as she stood.

"I can give you a ride home," Adam said as he gripped the back of a chair.

"I'm fine, really." She headed for the edge of the building, but he fell into step next to her.

"I'll at least walk you to your car."

"That's not necessary." Him being nice and caring

threatened to give her whiplash. It hinted at another layer of Adam, one that tempted her even more than she already was when she looked at him.

"Listen, you just took a full-out punch from a dude at least twice your size. I can tell you that if I took a punch from someone twice my size, I'd be a little woozy."

"You think I'm going to keel over between here and the parking lot?"

"Probably not, but falling face-first into the sand and suffocating sure would be a sucky way to go, wouldn't it?"

She would have laughed if she didn't suspect it would hurt. "True."

"Plus, it's not like I'm needed here at the moment." He gestured toward the nearly empty bar. The fight had sent all of the Beach Bum's customers fleeing.

"Looks like you might as well close for the night."

Suz walked by with her hands full of broken beer bottles. "Oh, don't worry, that's exactly what we're doing. I don't get paid enough to put up with that crap."

"Be back in a few," Adam said over his shoulder as he held Sara's elbow, helping her down to the sandy ground outside the bar.

Too tired to argue, Sara allowed him to walk her to the parking lot. Trudging through the sand took more effort than normal, and the image Adam had painted of her planting her face in that sand felt like a real possibility a couple of times. Her legs went noodley as they climbed the stairs to the wooden walk over the dunes, but she managed to stay upright.

When they reached her car, she tried to lower the ice pack to thank him.

He guided it back to her cheek. "You want to keep this on. Trust me."

"Had a few punches in your time?" She tried to ignore the warmth, the strength, the manly roughness of his palm cradling her hand.

"A few."

She couldn't help a laugh at what was obviously an understatement, but as she'd suspected it only hurt her pounding cheek more.

"You sure I can't drive you home?" he asked, all seriousness.

She resisted the urge to give in and let him, to allow herself to soak in his concern. "I'll be okay, but thanks."

He nodded and took a couple of steps back so she could open her car door. Her hand felt almost as cold as the ice at the absence of his warm touch. She nearly caved and told him she'd reconsidered just so she could stay in his presence a little longer. Instead, she got in the car and drove from the parking lot. But as she tried to drive with one hand and hold the ice pack to her face with the other, she wondered if she should have taken him up on his offer.

A zing of excitement shot through her at the idea. Frustrated by her traitorous body, she pitched the half-melted ice pack onto the floor of the passenger side.

Once again, she had to remind herself that Adam Canfield had *bad idea* written all over him—no matter how many times he rushed to the rescue. He'd probably already forgotten about her and gone in search of the blonde.

She turned off the main road onto her street and thought of her girls. Lilly had been abandoned at the hospital hours after her birth, so she'd never even known her parents. But Sara wasn't sure that wasn't better than what Tana had endured—having her parents flee the country without her to avoid drug trafficking charges.

As it always did, thinking about the girls' pasts brought up images of her own mother from the days before she'd walked away from her daughter and husband.

Sara shook her head despite how it made her jaw ache. She'd never understand how a parent could abandon a child. Her mother's abandonment fueled her own desire to be a good mother. And her father's efforts to be two parents in one had given Sara the type of role model she wanted for her own girls. Even if that type of person existed somewhere inside Adam Canfield, it would take too much effort to excavate it.

ADAM RETURNED TO the bar and got to work helping Suz clean up the mess. He slammed chairs back into their upright positions and tossed broken glass into the trash with more force than necessary so his body wouldn't give in to the shaking that threatened to overtake him. The same shaking he'd experienced after pulling that kid from the surf. That tormented him every time he woke up from a dream about Jessica.

He nearly crushed the back of a chair beneath his fists, wishing he'd never met Sara. Even if she'd only kept her distance, maybe he wouldn't be assaulted with thoughts and worries about yet another woman who put herself in the path of danger every single day, even when she wasn't on duty.

"You really like her, don't you?" Suz asked.

Adam ripped himself from his memories to look at Suz. "Who?"

She leaned back against the front of the long bar. "Well, not the blonde you were using all night to ignore the woman you really wanted to be with."

He waved off her assessment. "Just don't like jackasses hitting women and making a mess of things." He slammed a broken beer bottle into the trash, making it shatter into even more pieces.

"You forget I know you. That happens when I see your sorry ass every day. You were watching Sara all night."

He shoved the trash can back behind the bar. "Did you get knocked in the head, too?"

Suz shook her head. "Dude, one of these days you're going to have to settle for one of them. Otherwise, you'll turn into a dirty old man."

He didn't respond. In fact, they didn't speak to each other again until after they'd lowered the wooden sides of the building and secured all the locks for the night. And then it was only to say goodnight.

Hell. First, he'd had to deal with his unwanted feelings toward Sara. Then the stupid fight and its aftermath, reopening psychological scars he didn't even like admitting to himself existed. To top it off, Suz had decided to play shrink/matchmaker. It all added up to a nasty mood that unfortunately followed him all the way home like Pigpen's cloud.

He really needed to take out some aggression on his punching bag so that he didn't do something to get himself arrested, too. Though that might give him access to the bastard who'd hit Sara. Damn, he hated when the world insisted on poking holes in his carefree life. Wasn't it enough that his dreams haunted him?

His horoscope must be garbage for the month because when he pulled in to his driveway, his headlights illuminated a boy in his carport filling a water jug at the spigot on the side of the house.

The boy jumped at the unexpected arrival, and stared for a moment before he dropped the jug and ran.

Adam let a few choice words fly as he surged from his car and ran after the kid. Though the little brat had a head start, Adam managed to catch him at the back edge of the lot. The water thief struggled, but Adam was bigger, stronger, and it only took a moment to grip his arms tightly and make it abundantly clear that he wasn't going to make a brilliant escape.

"Let me guess. You're David Taylor."

The kid's eyes went so wide with fear that it punched Adam in the gut. His question to Sara the day she'd come to the bar with David's photo shot through his head, and he wondered again what the kid was running from.

David struggled against the grip of Adam's hands around his upper arms. "Let me go." His voice cracked, as if he was on the verge of tears and ashamed of it.

Adam gripped tighter, but not enough to hurt the boy, and shook him a little. "Hey, calm down. I'm not going to hurt you."

"I'm sorry about the water."

"Kid, that amount of water cost me about half a penny. I think I can manage it."

David looked up at him with a whirl of mistrust and questions in his eyes.

"Come on, let's go in and talk for a minute,"

Adam said as he guided David back toward the house. "I might even scrounge up enough stuff to make a sandwich."

If the kid was stealing water, chances were he was pretty darn hungry, too. His arm did feel scrawny under Adam's fingers, so he loosened his grip. He didn't want to bruise him.

Once inside, Adam nudged David toward the small kitchen table. "Sit."

David complied, but Adam could see the war taking place between making a getaway and yearning for the sandwich. Something about this scared, hungry boy gnawed at him.

Adam didn't question David. In fact, he said nothing as he pulled ham, cheese and mayo from the fridge and slapped together a sandwich, tossed it onto a paper towel and retrieved a new bag of barbecue chips from the cabinet. David sat on the edge of the chair eyeing Adam as he approached with the food. He didn't look away when Adam placed the sandwich and chips in front of him, even though his stomach growled at the proximity of the food.

"Go on, eat." Adam went to the fridge and retrieved a Coke.

When he turned back toward his unexpected guest, David had already scarfed down half of the sandwich and ripped into the bag of chips like he hadn't eaten in days. Damn, what had made this kid feel his only option was running away and nearly starving?

Fatigue like he hadn't known since his army days weighed down on Adam. As he made another sandwich for David, he realized that neither of them was up for any great conversation tonight. It was late. What could the cops do tonight anyway? What would it hurt to let the kid enjoy a decent night's sleep before contacting the authorities?

He slid the second sandwich onto the table just as David took the last bite of the first one. Adam sank into a chair adjacent to David's. The boy stiffened in response and stopped chewing.

"I'll make you a deal. I'm beat. You're probably dog tired, too. So what do you say we both just get some sleep?"

David's muscles tightened in the way of someone about to flee.

"I won't report you to the cops tonight if you sleep on the couch and promise not to run."

David still eyed him with suspicion, as if he thought he might be some pervert.

"Listen, kid, I've been working for what feels like a week straight, so I'm going to bed. You're welcome to whatever food you can find, but if I hear that door open, I'm calling the cops."

Still without speaking, David nodded.

"Good." Adam managed to drag his tired body to the bathroom before heading to bed.

His time in the bathroom amounted to about a minute, but by the time he returned to the hallway, David was already stretched out on the couch asleep. Adam shook his head. Poor kid. He was glad he'd given the boy a brief reprieve. Tomorrow was soon enough to deal with what to do with him.

He grabbed a blanket from his bedroom and placed it over David. Adam watched him sleep for a moment and thought back to the year he'd been fourteen. He would have rather slept on a complete stranger's couch, too.

HER LAUGHTER AT the driver's dirty joke made Adam smile. Their group, riding along the desert road in the Humvee, looked like one of those "Which item doesn't belong?" games. Three big army guys in camo, armed with guns and ammo galore, who liked to tell jokes in all shades of the blue spectrum and a petite, blonde aid worker with a heart the size of her home state of Texas.

She was doing a number on his heart, too. He wondered sometimes if the lack of women who weren't wearing as much camo and armament as him or donned in burqas was why he couldn't get her out of his mind. He doubted it. Hadn't been able to during the entire month he and his unit had escorted her and her fellow aid workers to sites outside of Baghdad. If he'd met Jessica back home, she would have spun him for a loop there, too. Fighting gun battles were nothing compared to trying to keep his hands off her as she sat in front of him. Irrational jealousy that Art, the driver, got to sit next to her flowed through Adam.

"I can do you one better than that," Jessica said as the hot wind whipped through the Humvee and caused tendrils of her honey-blond hair to fly about her flushed and slightly smudged face. She started to tell a dirty joke of her own, much to his disbelief.

Fate interrupted. Instead of a joke, what came out of Jessica was a scream. Adam reached for her as the Humvee went airborne and flew backward. But searing pain engulfed his leg. He screamed then froze as his eyes locked with the sightless ones on Jessica's bloody face. He screamed again as the world went black.

Adam shot up in bed, breathing hard, his throat raw at the remembered scream that had ripped from him a world away. He cursed and punched the mattress. Why the hell did he have to keep having the dreams?

Because you didn't keep her safe.

Adam cursed again and threw the sheet off his sweaty body. Why did that accusation always haunt him? What could he have done besides insist it was too dangerous for her to come along? Well, that hadn't exactly been his call, had it?

He'd made his point and been overruled.

He felt like punching holes in the wall, to punish himself again and again for not having been stronger in his opposition. Yes, it was some nut-job militant who'd put that roadside bomb in their path, but he couldn't shake the conviction that he'd had a duty to keep her safe and he'd failed.

Sweat trickled down his forehead. He swiped at it then headed for the bathroom to wash his face. He knew better than to try going back to sleep immediately. The dream would just come back, as if he'd hit the pause button on a DVD player. If he could have the part of his brain that remembered Iraq surgically removed, he'd do it without a second thought.

Snoring from the couch told him that David hadn't bolted. Adam hoped he had enough food in the fridge to make the kid a decent breakfast in the morning.

In the bathroom, he ran cold water and splashed his face. Still dripping, he looked at his shadowed image in the partially lit room. Fatigue hit him anew, and it had nothing to do with the hours he'd worked. No, this was the type of exhaustion that came from keeping up the front, trying to make everyone, including himself, believe he was just a happy-go-lucky, not-a-care-in-the-world beach lounger. God, how he wished it were true beyond the surface.

He shoved away from the sink and wandered back into the hallway.

Normally, after a dream he'd watch a little TV to fill his head with other images, but he didn't want to wake David. Though it was possible the kid was so tired he wouldn't even wake up.

Adam eased into the living room and stopped when he saw how David was sleeping. Curled into the fetal position with his hands protecting his head.

Flaming, dangerous anger lit inside Adam. A teenage boy wouldn't sleep like that without a reason, unless he felt he was in danger.

God help the person who'd put that type of fear in the boy.

Chapter Five

Adam didn't sleep the rest of the night. Instead, he sat on the side of his bed thinking, trying to decide the best course of action. As the sun rose on another gorgeous Gulf Coast day, he corraled the three eggs and two pieces of bacon left in the fridge and fixed them with some toast. He placed the plate of food, a half jar of grape jelly, silverware and a mug of coffee on the table before David ever stirred.

Adam guessed the boy had slept about as much as he'd eaten since he'd run off from home.

Finally, David rolled over on the couch then came awake with such a jerk that he ended up halfway on the floor.

"Watch the coffee table. An elephant could dance on that thing, so I'm guessing it'd leave a mark if you hit it." Adam kept his words casual and friendly, in a teasing sort of way. He needed David to feel comfortable so he'd agree to what Adam had finally decided to do in the early morning hours. "Come on and eat before it gets cold."

David straightened his rumpled T-shirt as he got up and slowly approached the table. He eyed the hot food, but then he looked back at Adam.

"You call the cops?"

"No."

"Why not?"

"Because I said I wouldn't yet."

David glanced at the food again.

"Go on." Adam nodded toward the meal as he took a long drink of black coffee.

David slid into the chair he'd sat in the night before and took several bites before meeting Adam's eyes again. "Why are you helping me?"

Adam shrugged. "Looked like you could use it."

"I can take care of myself," David said, all teen-age bravado.

"No doubt."

They occupied their opposite sides of the kitchen, David at the table, Adam leaning against the counter next to the coffeepot, for several minutes. Finally, Adam filled his thermos with coffee and walked to the end of the bar separating the kitchen from the living room.

"I've got to go to work, so here's the deal. You can stay here today, but don't go outside." He didn't want to send the kid back to a bad home, but he didn't want to be arrested for harboring a runaway, either. He just wanted to give David a chance to tell him why he'd run away. Adam needed to figure out what would happen to David if he turned him over to the authorities.

Damn, the entire situation reeked of responsibility, but what was he supposed to do? Call the police and have the kid possibly end up back where someone made him feel he had to protect himself as he slept? That was no way for a kid to live.

"That sound okay to you?" Adam asked.

David nodded. Adam gave a quick nod back then headed out the front door. They'd have to talk later, but Adam didn't know exactly what to say. He needed the day to think it through. Plus, David didn't appear to be ready to do the sharing thing yet, but hopefully he'd open up after a day of relative safety. Adam paused before opening the door. "I'm Adam, by the way. I work down at the pier, just in case you need to know."

As he drove to work, a new devil poked his pitchfork into him. The thought that if Sara knew what he was doing, she wouldn't like it—or him—one little bit.

SARA STARED IN the mirror the morning after the bar fight, gently examining the ugly bruise on her face. She winced at the tenderness. Geez, she looked like one of the battered women she'd helped over the years.

"Hope the other guy looks worse," Tana said from where she stood in the doorway to the bathroom, one hand propped against the door frame.

"Meeting violence with violence isn't the best answer," Sara said, trying to sound firm but not preachy. Through trial and error, she'd found that reaching a teenager required a certain type of non-confrontational approach. They wanted to be talked *to,* not *at.*

But, even as she said the words, she was pretty sure the other guy looked worse this morning. He'd taken a beer bottle upside the head, as well as several punches.

"Your breakfast is ready," Tana said, then disappeared from the doorway.

Sara did her best to cover up the bruise, but it was a lost cause. She ran a brush through her hair and headed for the kitchen. An English muffin topped with strawberry jam and a cup of coffee greeted her.

"Mornin', Mommy," Lilly said and smiled wide, as usual.

"Good morning, sweetie-pie," Sara said as she leaned down to hug her daughter. "You are the smiliest girl in the whole world."

"Ugh, morning people," Tana grumbled from where she was pouring a bowl of cereal for Lilly.

"Ignore your sister," Sara said to Lilly and rubbed her nose against the little girl's.

Lilly barely touched her fingertip to Sara's bruised cheek. "You have a big owie."

"Yep, Mommy ran into something at work. But

it's okay." If you counted throbbing and making her wish her cheek would fall off okay.

A knock at the door sent Lilly flying.

"Remember to ask who it is," Sara called after her.

"Who is it?" Lilly asked in a singsongy voice, knowing full well it was likely Ruby come to pick up her and Tana.

"It's the Wicked Witch of the West," Ruby said through the door, making Lilly giggle.

Sara shook her head and smiled. Ruby, despite her age putting her firmly in the grandma years, acted as young as Lilly sometimes.

"Good glorious morning, all," Ruby said as she entered the kitchen. She caught sight of Sara's face and grimaced. "Okay, maybe not for all. What happened to you?"

"Wee disagreement among drinking buddies got out of hand at the Beach Bum."

Ruby examined the bruise a bit more closely. "Girl, I think dating might be safer on your next night off."

Sara snorted and pointed toward her proof of fisticuffs. "I don't think I'll be attracting any men anytime soon."

"I don't think Adam would mind," Tana said, mischief in her voice.

"Who's Adam?" Ruby asked.

Sara gave Tana the evil eye, which only made her smile her "Ha, ha, I got you" smile.

"No one," Sara answered Ruby.

"He's this totally good-looking guy Mom met when she had to investigate a prowler at his house."

Ruby shoved her tanned hands into the pockets of her white capri pants. "Do tell."

Tana started to speak, but Sara jumped in before she could get a word out. "Contrary to Tana's wild imagination, there is nothing to tell. It was Adam Canfield."

"Oh, he is easy on the eyes."

"And knows it," Sara mumbled.

"There was definite sparkage going on between them," Tana said, amusement in her words.

Sara's mouth fell open before she caught herself. "Tana, don't lie!"

"I'm not. I may be thirteen, but I'm not blind."

Sara rolled her eyes and sighed in exasperation. She took a long drink of coffee and dreaded the next few years of hormonal teenage girl.

"He'd be a catch if someone managed to do it," Ruby said with an eye twinkle of her own.

"Yeah, he's a real catch. He 'works' at the pier and hangs out at the Beach Bum as his main form of recreation."

"So he's a laid-back type of guy. Too many up-tight people in the world, if you ask me."

Sara looked at Ruby. Did the older woman think Sara was among the uptight throng?

"You should ask him to the Helping Hands Ball," Tana said, her voice going up in excitement.

"I think not."

"Why not?" Tana asked.

"Because he's not the type of guy I'm looking for, okay, Miss Pushy. Now go get ready for school."

Tana might be getting old enough to notice guys, but Sara didn't feel like trying to explain how she didn't want to let herself think about Adam in a romantic way. She tended to care for a guy too easily, and she didn't want to fall for someone who would only end up hurting her. She'd seen how it had hurt her father.

Tana threw her hands up in exasperation then headed for her room.

Lilly tired of the grown-up conversation and took her doll into the living room and parked herself in front of the Cartoon Network.

"I think a date with Adam might work out better for you than drinks with coworkers," Ruby said as she gestured toward Sara's bruise.

Sara turned and poured the last few drops of her coffee down the sink and rinsed the cup. "He's good-looking, yes. Looks aren't important though when compared to other attributes."

"He saved a child's life."

"I'm aware of that." As if that negated the entire con column about dating him.

She walked past Ruby and ushered the girls toward the door. "Come on, I've got to get to work."

The girls went out the door, but Ruby paused

before stepping over the threshold. She nodded toward Sara's collection of classic TV shows on DVD. *The Andy Griffith Show*. *Little House on the Prairie*. *The Waltons*.

"You need to stop looking for Mr. Perfect because he doesn't exist. He's fiction. If you keep passing up real guys for the myth, you're going to grow old alone. And trust me, you don't want to do that."

It was the first time Sara had ever heard Ruby express any sort of hint of dissatisfaction with her life.

"I just don't think he's the sort of guy for me. You know his reputation."

"It's a date, Sara." Ruby squeezed Sara's hand. "Stop pressuring yourself to find the perfect daddy for those girls. And stop thinking that taking time for yourself in some way makes you a bad mother. You need space." She nodded in the direction the girls had taken. "They need space."

With that, Ruby made her exit, leaving Sara searching for a response that never came. Slowly, she closed the door and leaned against it. Adam was delicious…

"Arrggh," she said and pushed away from the door. She couldn't let Ruby and Tana's tag-team matchmaking get to her. There was a perfect guy for her, she knew it. She only had to find him.

She hurried to her room for her badge, gun and car keys. When she picked up her badge from the top of the dresser, she glanced at her marred face in the mirror. Ruby's words played over in her head, then the events of the night before. How her coworkers had tried to tease her and instead of admitting that she was attracted to Adam, she'd felt the need to deny it. Sure, that made sense if she wanted to maintain good working relationships and keep the guys from treating her as if she was frail, but it didn't do anything to help her shaky self-esteem as a woman.

She sighed and slowly ran her fingers over her face. It hit her anew how much she'd missed out on by not having a mother or sisters to teach her how to be beautiful, feminine, sexy. Sometimes she felt like she didn't belong in the female world or the male one. She existed somewhere in between, always waging a constant battle with herself over which way to go. Sure, she had pretty clothes and jewelry, but she was always so self-conscious about wearing it, fearing she'd look like a fake.

With a sigh, she left the mirror and her house behind. She needed the cases sitting on her desk to take her mind off these things that didn't matter. Helping find David Taylor, raising her daughters to know how much she loved them, not lowering her standards—those were the things that mattered. Not all the things she could fantasize doing with Adam Canfield.

Despite her determination to not think about Adam, snippets of the night before kept replaying in her mind. Considering how he'd taken care of her, how much he'd seemed concerned about her well-being, maybe he wasn't such a bad guy after all. In fact, she half expected him to call and check on her.

Or was that thought as crazy as the belief her father had always harbored that his wife, Sara's mother, would someday come back to them?

SARA CAUGHT HERSELF staring at the phone much too often, but Adam didn't call. Which just proved she'd been right to begin with.

But then why did she find herself being upset or annoyed when she should be focusing on following up on case leads or out canvassing the area for David Taylor?

She decided not to delve into examining the reasons too closely. Instead, she redoubled her efforts at work and planned to spend some extra quality time with the girls. She would put a stop to Ruby's matchmaking. Maybe she could forget Adam Canfield if she made sure she didn't see him.

Of course, the size of Horizon Beach was working against her. She couldn't very well push thoughts of him away when she ran into him at Wal-Mart after work. The pale green T-shirt he wore showcased his tan and the green hue of his eyes. It was a miracle every woman in the store wasn't following him from aisle to aisle.

She spotted him in the cereal aisle before he saw

her and nearly made like a coward and retraced her steps. Okay, that was just stupid. History proved that she was going to run into him from time to time. Besides, if he meant nothing, why did it matter if she spoke to him next to the Frosted Flakes?

"Hey," she said, affecting a casualness she wished she actually felt.

"Hey. Oh, ow." He glanced at her cheek. "You were right. Nice shiner."

"Yes, I think everyone in town has made exactly the same comment."

"It'll be gone before you know it."

"I hope so. I'm just sorry I didn't get in a good punch myself." She couldn't admit that to Tana, of course.

A woman trailed by with four kids in tow, all of whom were pleading for different kinds of cereal, causing Sara to push her cart closer to Adam's. She noticed the amount of food in his.

"Did you come to the store hungry?"

"What?" He looked at her and then at the contents of his shopping cart filled with chips, cookies, bacon, eggs, 24-packs of Coke. "Uh, just haven't been in awhile. Don't like shopping." He backed his cart away from hers. "I've about had my limit, so I'll see you later."

She stood in the aisle listening to the continuing debate about which cereal had the best prize as she watched Adam flee. What the...? Surely she wasn't that scary-looking. She eyed a box of fudge-covered Oreos at the end of the aisle. The perfect pouting food.

She took a couple of steps before a wave of frustration engulfed her. She wasn't a chicken, so why did this man make her feel as though she was acting like one? She turned her cart around and hurried up the aisle past the frustrated mother who now had three types of cereal in her cart.

"Adam?"

At first, she thought he either didn't hear her or was playing the ignoring game for some reason. But after a couple of steps, he stopped and turned, if a bit hesitantly.

What did she say now that she had his attention again?

"Hey, I've got to make an appearance at this police/fire department benefit thing. Would you like to go?"

His eyes widened, and he tilted his head slightly. "With you?"

A wave of nervousness made her question her sanity. Had she just done the most embarrassing thing in her life only to be shot down in the cereal aisle? She snatched some snarkiness from the recirculated air around her. "Well, I guess you could go with the chief. He's a nice-looking guy, but it is Horizon Beach. People might talk."

"Think I'll pass, thanks."

Part of her had expected the rejection, but when it came she wasn't prepared for the kick to her heart. How could her heart be involved? She barely knew the guy. She should walk away before he did.

"Pass on the chief, that is."

It took a moment for her to pull herself out of her backpedaling plans to put a cap on her sudden excitement. "So you do want to go?"

"Sure." He didn't exactly sound like it was going to be the highlight of his life, but he hadn't rejected her. That was enough.

"Good." What did she say now to fill the awkward silence? "You might come in handy if too much liquor flows and punches start flying." She smiled, and it only felt a little forced.

"I'll make sure the bartenders have ice packs at the ready." With that and a mischievous smile, he gripped the cart handle, ready to leave. "Just let me know the details."

"Okay." She stood and watched him disappear around the corner, heading for the shortest checkout line, before turning her own cart and running the gauntlet of cereal again. The mom and begging children had vacated the aisle, so she allowed a smile to stretch across her face. She did, however, stop herself from doing the happy dance or analyzing why his "yes" had made her so happy.

When she reached the end of the aisle, she snatched the fudge-covered Oreos and tossed them in the cart. Now they weren't sulking cookies. They were celebratory cookies.

She managed to keep her composure during the rest of her shopping, all through the checkout process, all the way until she sat in the driver's seat of her car. Only then did she allow herself a squeal and a bit of a celebration. The thought of dancing in Adam's arms, even if it led to absolutely nothing beyond that night—and it couldn't—gave her a giddiness high not unlike that of a teenage girl.

Her wide smile froze and drained away, however, when she glanced in the rearview mirror and saw the purple marring her face. She stared at herself as the panic set in. Full-blown, nuclear-reactor-alarms-going-off panic. What had she been thinking? How would she ever make herself look as good as the beautiful women she always saw on Adam's arm? She couldn't, no matter how many cosmetics, hair products and stylish clothes she employed.

She shook her head at her foolishness, not for having asked him, but for worrying about suddenly transforming herself into eye candy. She didn't have to. She told herself what she would likely have to tell Tana soon—to just be herself, and if that wasn't enough then the guy wasn't the right one for her.

And she knew, deep down, that Adam wasn't. He was only a date, a diversion, a body to keep her from attending the benefit alone. Not the Mr. Perfect she longed to find.

Chapter Six

Adam stopped himself from honking at the person in front of him, an older man taking too long to start rolling after the stoplight turned green. He wanted to get home, unload all these groceries before they started sending up a beacon saying, "I'm buying all this food for a hungry boy who happens to be a runaway hiding in my house."

When the old man took an eternity to turn in to the parking lot for the medical clinic, Adam gritted his teeth to keep from roaring like a lion.

He wondered when exactly he'd lost his mind.

Not only was he harboring a runaway on gut instinct, voluntarily making himself responsible for the kid, but now he'd also agreed to go out with Sara. A woman who'd already proven right in front of him that her job put her in danger for "the greater good." A woman who could arrest his ass if she found out about David.

Maybe he'd been gassed with some "lose your

common sense" agent while he'd been kicking up dust in the desert.

At the last possible moment, he whipped his car in to the parking area for one of the half-dozen sections of Gulf Islands National Seashore that dotted the Gulf Coast. He watched a couple of bright-white fishing boats motor across Choctawhatchee Bay.

Damn it. Why had he said yes to her invitation? It only promised to add to his mounting headaches.

Because for some reason he couldn't stop thinking about her. Was it simply because she'd never acted like other women around him? Even that first time they'd met months ago, before he'd known she was a cop, she hadn't succumbed to his flirting like most women. He hoped a date and maybe some kissing was enough to get her out of his system. He needed her to do something to totally turn off his insane attraction. But before that, he needed for David to open up to say he was just being bratty and go back to a loving family.

Adam sighed as he watched the wake of the fishing boats lap against the sandy shore. No matter how much he wanted them to, he didn't believe either of those scenarios was going to happen.

He guessed he should just be thankful that beyond the extra food in his shopping cart, Sara hadn't noticed the clothes to fit a fourteen-year-old boy. He still couldn't believe he'd taken yet another step tying him to David, to being responsible for someone else's well-being. But the kid looked like he'd been wearing the same T-shirt and jeans for days. The fact David hadn't taken the time to pack didn't give Adam a good feeling about what the kid had been through.

Even though he'd just bought more groceries than he ever had, Adam stopped by Freddie's and picked up a supreme pizza. If he tried to cook in his current mood, he'd probably burn everything or catch the house on fire.

When he pulled in to his driveway and cut the car's engine, he grabbed the pizza and the two bags filled with things that needed to be refrigerated.

He stepped through the front door only to stop cold. Everything looked different, smelled different. It looked and smelled...clean.

Adam closed the door behind him. "Did I win the Merry Maids lotto or something?"

David, who was in the process of shoving the broom back in the closet where it spent most of its time, stared at him as if he might be punished. "I just thought I'd clean. I was bored and..." He swallowed visibly. "It's the least I can do after you gave me a place to stay last night. I hope you don't mind."

God, the kid was always so on edge, like he fully expected Adam's mood to suddenly turn angry.

"Mind? Kid, I might just hire you."

David grinned at that, the first time Adam had

seen anything resembling happiness on his face. His gut twisted that such a simple, teasing few words was all it took to make the kid smile. It made him dread the conversation they would have to have tonight. Truth be told, he'd rather avoid it. He suspected that down that path lay heavier stuff than he wanted to hear. Damn, he hated the heavy. He watched as his life plan to avoid it for the rest of his days derailed right in front of him.

He slid the pizza box onto the clean coffee table then deposited the contents of the bags in the fridge. He grabbed a couple of Cokes and headed for the couch. "Let's eat while it's still hot. I've been craving Freddie's pizza all day."

They dug in, each losing himself in the ecstasy of gooey cheese, spicy pepperoni and the other wonders of a piping-hot pizza. Each had downed two pieces before Adam tackled the dreaded subject.

"What made you run away?"

David, who'd been reaching for a third slice, pulled his hand back and didn't respond beyond a shrug. Adam could almost feel the boy curling in on himself, planning to make another getaway.

Adam didn't push. It wouldn't do any good. The kid would share when he was ready, if he ever was. It wasn't like Adam had ever gone around crying about his dad's temper and refusal to say anything nice about his wife and son.

He decided to give it a little more time and clicked

on a baseball game. The Marlins were already down three runs in the second inning. They watched in silence. Adam ate another slice of pizza, but David didn't move. The second inning flowed into the third and then the fourth.

When the Marlins batter popped one into right field and a teammate stole two bases to score, Adam whooped. "That's more like it."

He glanced over at David, who sat staring at the TV but offering no reaction to the play. Adam returned his attention to the TV.

"My dad makes me steal," David said.

Adam didn't turn off the TV, didn't even turn toward David. He sensed that doing so would cause the boy to clam up again. "What did you steal?"

"Tools, bikes, anything he could sell. Shoplifted for food sometimes."

"And you got tired of it?"

"I almost got caught by one of our neighbors." He made a disgusted sound. "She's a nice lady, friendly. I hated myself for stealing from her, so I put the stuff back."

"Your dad got mad at you for that?"

"I didn't go back home. That's when I left."

That explained why he had nothing but the clothes on his back. Though Adam suspected he'd had precious little at home to pack anyway.

"I knew if I went back, he'd beat me again," David said, so matter-of-fact that Adam had to force himself not to curl his hands into fists. The guy deserved a dose of what he dished out, and Adam was willing to do the dishing.

"He beat you a lot?"

David shrugged. "When he thought I didn't bring home enough stuff."

Adam shifted slightly so he could see the expression on David's face. It reflected one part hatred, one part scared little boy.

"Didn't anyone notice?" Why hadn't anyone done anything?

"He knows where to hit so it doesn't show." David took a deep, shaky breath, then let it out in a slow exhale. "He said if I ever showed anyone the bruises, I'd wish I hadn't."

Adam tried to fill his next question with concern, not the boiling anger he was really feeling. "What about your mom?"

David leaned forward and picked at the edge of a piece of pizza. "She died when I was three, killed herself by driving off a bridge on I-10."

Adam couldn't help the curse he uttered. "I'm sorry."

Again with the "that's just the way it is" shrug. David pulled his hand back a second time. "Thank you for letting me crash here last night. I probably need to be going now."

"Not gonna happen," Adam said, surprising himself with the conviction behind his words.

"If you call the cops, they'll send me back. I'm not going back."

"No, you're not." Adam looked down at his fisted hand and forced himself to relax. "Listen, I know the detective who is working your case. She's a good cop, loves kids. She wouldn't let anything happen to you."

David's body tensed, on the verge of fleeing. Adam stayed him by placing his hand atop the boy's forearm. "You can't keep running. It's too dangerous. Maybe if you were close to eighteen already it'd be different, but you're not. How are you going to live for the next four years?"

"I'll manage."

"By stealing?"

David froze then slumped forward with his head in his hands. "Can't I just stay here? I promise I won't be any trouble. I'll work to pay for my food."

"Kid, trust me, I'm the last person you want to live with." Adam fought the urge to agree to David's suggestion despite the impossibility of that situation and how much being responsible for a kid freaked him out. "Plus, you need to be in school, live with a real family."

Adam sat back and watched some more of the game, letting David have time to think about what he'd said.

When the game broke for a commercial, David sighed. "Okay."

Adam's heart squeezed at the weary acceptance in that single word. Still, he nodded and headed for the phone. As he looked up and dialed Sara's home number, he hated the feeling that he was betraying the kid.

SARA STILL COULDN'T believe she'd asked Adam to the benefit. Part of her thought she'd taken leave of her senses while another was jumping up and down like she'd just been asked to the prom by the cutest boy in school.

When the phone rang, she reached for it automatically, not because she was actually thinking he'd call.

"Hello?"

"Sara, it's Adam."

Her heart thumped harder, and her first thought was that he was calling to cancel. He'd remembered in the minutes after leaving the store that he didn't like cops, she was a cop and therefore he couldn't possibly go with her.

"Hey," was all she could manage to say.

"I don't know how to do this, but I need to meet you somewhere. Maybe the police station."

"What's wrong?"

He exhaled. "I need to bring David Taylor to you."

"David Taylor?"

"Yeah, I caught the kid getting some water from the spigot on the side of the house."

"Is he okay?"

"Yeah. He was hungry so I fed him." Adam

lowered his voice. "He had a good reason for leaving, and I told him you wouldn't send him back."

"Why would you promise that?"

"I told him you were a good person, loved kids. He's been abused."

Disgust and anger made tears spring to her eyes. "Okay, bring him to the station. I'll be there in a few minutes."

After calling Ruby to watch the girls again, she hurried back to work and pulled out David's file before Adam walked in beside a nervous-looking David Taylor. She offered the boy a big smile.

"Hello, David," she said as she offered her hand. "Nice to meet you."

David hesitated before taking her hand in his and shaking it. Her heart ached for this kid—part boy, part man—and the fear and strength warring in his eyes.

Sara glanced at Adam. "Let's all go to the conference room. A friend of mine from Social Services, Lara Stephens, is on her way." When she saw David stiffen, she gently placed her hand on his shoulder and guided him toward the conference room across from her desk.

Adam grabbed her wrist, drawing her attention to him as David walked into the conference room.

"He really doesn't need to go back home. He told me his dad made him steal, and when it wasn't enough he knew how to hit the kid so no one noticed."

Sara's stomach rolled, and determination that David would never have to fear his father again welled within her. "I'll do everything I can. Thanks for bringing him in."

Adam nodded but didn't look like he was going to follow her into the room.

She lowered her voice so David couldn't hear. "I think it'd be good if you came in. If he's comfortable enough to tell you about the abuse, it might help him to have you sitting beside him."

The desire to flee sparked in his eyes, but he nodded and followed her into the room. Sara got cups of water for all of them while they waited for Lara to arrive. After introductions were made again, Sara caught Adam's eyes and saw how anxious he was. Best to get the interview over with as quickly as possible.

"David, I need you to tell me what happened that made you feel you had to run away from home."

David looked at Adam, who nodded. As David explained his home situation, Sara took notes and occasionally glanced at Adam. He didn't say anything, but his mere presence seemed to help David get through the disturbing details of his relationship with his father.

When she finished the questioning, Sara closed her folder. "You'll be going with Lara now. She'll make sure you have what you need and place you in a temporary foster home until we work everything out, okay?"

David merely nodded. As they all rose, Adam squeezed David's shoulder. She was left with the impression he was trying to give the boy strength to carry on, and it melted her heart a little.

Sara stood in the area outside the conference room, watching as Lara accompanied David out of the building. "Thanks for taking care of him," she said. "I'm relieved he's okay."

"You were good with him."

She shrugged and headed toward her desk. "Kids who run away are usually skittish. They're hurting or scared, feel like they're alone in the world."

"You've dealt with lots of runaways?"

"Several. Too many," she said as she dropped David's case file atop her desk.

"Sounds like a hard job."

"Sometimes. But times like now feel good, when we find them alive and for the most part okay."

Adam glanced toward the now empty front entrance. "He won't have to go back to that bastard, right?"

"If everything he said checks out, no." She rubbed her temples, dreading the next part.

"What's wrong?"

"Now I get to call his father."

"I could just go beat the daylights out of him." He looked like nothing would give him more pleasure.

"Thanks for the offer, but I'm pretty sure they don't have happy hour at the jail."

He smiled at that, and she felt herself slip further under his spell. She had to get him out of here so she could think straight and do her job.

"I'll go so you can finish." His gaze met hers for a moment before he turned and headed for the door.

When he walked out of sight, she sank into her chair and took a deep breath. She steered her thoughts away from him and toward the task at hand, then reached for the phone.

SARA STARED INTO her closet an hour before the Helping Hands Ball was set to start, no idea what to wear. Why hadn't she made the time to go shopping? Maybe because she'd been sure the date wouldn't really happen. After all, she hadn't seen or talked to Adam in the week since he'd brought David to the station. Although Lara had told her he'd called David to check on him a couple of times.

She placed her hand against her upset stomach. Would anyone find her if she just stepped into the closet and hid in the corner until the night was over?

"Stop overthinking," Ruby said from the open doorway.

"Let me guess. Tana called you."

Ruby held up her thin, baby blue cell phone. "Texted me, actually."

"Texted?" There was something bone-deep funny about a little white-haired lady using abbreviations and emoticons to communicate.

"Yes. She's been showing me how to do that. She even set me up on Twitter. My granddaughters think it's hysterical when they get my updates. You know, I'm 'baking a pie' or 'weeding my flowerbeds.'"

Sara lifted her hand to her mouth to try to muffle a laugh but wasn't successful. "Okay, it is a little funny."

Ruby shrugged and slid the phone into her pocket. "Hey, just because I'm a granny doesn't mean I can't be hip."

Sara stifled a snort and the urge to hug Ruby for no apparent reason.

"Now, let's get you ready for this party." Ruby wandered into the room, followed by Tana. Lilly ran in and jumped up on the bed. She loved playing dress-up, so of course she was in on the conspiracy, as well.

Old insecurities combined forces with doubts about the wisdom of letting herself get closer to Adam. What if she found herself softening toward him more than she already had? What if she even let herself fall for him? She knew it wouldn't last and she'd just end up hurt.

"I'm tired. I think I'm going to cancel." Sara headed for the door to the hallway. Maybe she'd make cookies and watch a movie with the girls.

Ruby grabbed her by the wrist. "Oh, no you don't. You finally got up the nerve to ask that boy out, and you're going through with it."

"Why?" Sara's voice, against her will, held a note

of pleading. She wanted Ruby to say something that would convince her this was a good idea.

"Because it'll be fun," Ruby said.

"How do you know that?"

"I'm old. I know everything."

Both girls giggled. "Don't worry," Tana said. "We're going to fix you up. You'll blow Adam away."

"I seriously doubt that." But Sara gave up the fight in the face of three opponents. She'd let them do their best and hope she ended up passable. She'd done a lot harder things in her life than fumble her way through an ill-advised date. Like accepting she'd probably never see her own mother again.

She shook off the memories and allowed Ruby to pull clothes from the closet and hold them up to her. This went on, Ruby and Tana making remarks pro or con along the way, for a good five minutes until Ruby found a red, wraparound dress in the darkest corner of the closet.

"Oh, yeah, that's more like it," Tana said. "Good V-neck, flowy skirt, pretty."

"This will look wonderful with your dark coloring," Ruby added, then proceeded to dig in the floor of the closet. "Please tell me you have some shoes to go with that."

She hadn't worn the dress since a three-day cruise she'd taken the year before she'd come to Horizon Beach. Did she still have the shoes? She eyed the interior of the closet and spotted a shoebox under a duffel bag. "There." She pointed toward the box, and Ruby retrieved it.

Tana removed the cover and pulled out the red satin slingbacks. Sara could still hear the saleslady's voice as she'd waxed poetic about the shoe's "rounded peep toe" and "adorable pleat accent."

"Oh, pretty," Lilly said as her eyes grew wider.

While Tana toed the line between cute and trendy and walking anime/goth girl, Lilly was all girly-girl and hadn't met a bow or frill she didn't love with all of her little girl heart.

"Sara, I'm seeing a whole new side of you," Ruby said with a wicked grin.

"Those have been worn exactly once, on a cruise ship."

"Well, it's time we put them back into service. These shoes were made for dancing. Among other things." Ruby said the last part under her breath so only Sara could hear her.

Sara's mouth dropped open a little at the implication. "Ruby," she scolded. But she couldn't help the thrill of possibility that soared through her at the thought that Adam might think the same thing.

After Tana picked out jewelry she deemed appropriate, she and Ruby ushered Sara into the bathroom and made her sit on the closed toilet lid. For the next half hour, they brushed and curled and applied make-up like they were on a cable makeover show competing for fame and glory.

When they finally stood back and admired their handiwork, their mouths stretched with big, satisfied smiles. That had to be good, right?

Lilly scooted her way in front of them, stopped and stared. "Mommy, you're bootiful."

Sara choked up at her darling daughter's assessment. It had all been worth it even if when she looked in the mirror she looked like Tammy Faye Baker or Marilyn Manson. She kissed Lilly on the cheek then stood and turned toward the mirror.

"Oh." She couldn't believe the image staring back at her. She didn't look scary at all. She turned her face so that her bruised cheek was toward the mirror. She couldn't even see the discoloration. She bit her lip.

"Don't you dare cry and mess up our work," Ruby said.

"You like it?" Tana asked, some of her lovable snarkiness giving way to the need to please.

Sara turned away from her image in the mirror and hugged Tana close. "Yes. I think you two might be miracle workers."

"It's just makeup and hair product," Tana said. "You're already pretty."

"And I don't think we're going to be the only people to think so," Ruby said with satisfaction lighting her pale blue eyes.

The nervousness returned full force, and Sara brought her hand to her stomach again. "I think I'm going to be sick."

Ruby spun her around and pushed her toward the bedroom. "No, you're not. You're going to go and have a marvelous time."

WHEN SARA SPOTTED Adam outside the hotel ballroom, she thought maybe Ruby was right. Her breath caught at the sight of him dressed in a dark suit and tie. His shoulders looked wider, his eyes greener and more beckoning. He'd been good-looking before, but now he brought drop-dead gorgeous to new levels. And she wasn't the only person to notice. Other women, even plenty of married ones, watched him a little longer than necessary. She tried not to think about the possibility that he'd been with any of them before. She had to confine her thoughts to having fun this one night and nothing beyond that.

When he saw her, the way his eyes came to life as they widened and he froze in place as though he might trip if he took another step told her that Lilly was right. For tonight, at least, she looked beautiful.

For tonight, she was going to put concerns aside and enjoy herself. As Adam approached her, appreciation in his expression, her heart sped up. She almost licked her lips, but halted the action just in time, before she made it obvious how his appearance affected her.

"Detective Greene, you will cause wrecks in that dress. I'm not sure the public is safe." His teasing was low and sexy, making her skin tingle.

Heat rushed up her neck to her face. She hoped

the makeup hid the redness as well as it did the evidence of the bar brawl.

"And who knew there was a debonair man beyond the beach-lover," she teased right back.

"Guess we're both just full of surprises," he said as he offered his arm.

She swallowed and prayed that he couldn't feel how her body vibrated at his closeness. A whiff of some spicy scent—maybe shampoo, maybe after-shave—caused her to take a slow, deep breath. It served the dual purpose of calming her nerves and filling her senses with Adam's presence.

As he led her through the crowd, she noticed all eyes turning their way. Whether it was because of the man on her arm or the sight of her in a dress and "do me" heels, she had no idea. She tried to ignore the stares, but that proved impossible when she knew nearly everyone and had to say hello to them.

"You come to this every year?" Adam asked as he led her toward the bar at the far end of the ballroom.

"Yeah, it's kind of an unspoken expectation of the job."

"I'm guessing you've never worn that dress to this soiree before."

"Perceptive of you," she said as she spotted Shawn and Keith. Great, after she'd told them that night in the Beach Bum that she didn't like Adam. Why hadn't she thought about this eventuality?

"Damn, Greene," Shawn said when he saw her.

"I will never be able to look at you the same way again." His blue eyes swept over her body, pausing at her breasts.

"If you don't look at my face instead of the V-neck, you won't be able to look at anything past your swollen eyelids." She glanced around the room. "Where's Tanya, anyway?" Maybe he'd behave himself if his girlfriend was there to keep his eyeballs in the appropriate place.

"Ladies room."

"You do look nice, Sara," said Keith, a decade older and more of a gentleman than his cohort.

"Thanks. Keith Hutchens, Shawn Winters, this is Adam Canfield."

"From the Beach Bum, right?" Shawn asked, a hint of mischief in his question.

Sara narrowed her eyes at him. Shawn noted her look and tried to wipe the smile off his face.

"Had any more trouble?" Keith asked, perhaps fearing Sara was going to use one of her satin-covered stilettos to do Shawn bodily injury.

"Nah. Zac's home, so thankfully I'm back on the customer side of the bar now."

"Pretty good place to pick up the hotties," Shawn said.

Adam glanced at Sara and smiled. "A few have wandered through now and then."

This time, her entire body warmed, not just her neck and face. Something about the timbre of his voice, the way he looked at her, had her thinking of wrapping herself around him.

"Well, we'll see you guys later," she said. "I want to check out the silent auction items." She guided Adam away from her coworkers and tried to pretend no questioning gazes were turned in their direction.

As if he wanted to add to the gossip fire, Adam slid his hand around hers as they perused the items included in the silent auction. It felt so nice, so warm, so encompassing that she didn't pull away. It was just for tonight, she kept telling herself. If she only had to commit to one night, she wanted to soak up every pleasurable experience she could. Tomorrow, she'd deal with the fact that he'd probably be on to the next beautiful woman to cross his path.

Why did that make her sad?

Adam lifted a piece of stiff card stock that sat in front of a kangaroo figurine.

"What is it?" she asked, wondering if it was a valuable one-of-a-kind carving.

"Trip to Australia. Looks like it includes pretty much the entire continent, too." He offered her the card, and she read down the itinerary.

"Wow, this sounds fabulous. I've always been fascinated by Australia."

"Was it *Crocodile Dundee* or *The Thorn Birds* that did it for you?" Adam asked with a teasing grin.

"Actually, it was *Life in a Sunburned Country* by Bill Bryson."

He lifted his eyebrows like he didn't quite believe her. Something about his knowing expression made her confess all.

"Okay, so maybe *The Man from Snowy River* had something to do with it. And, uh, Hugh Jackman didn't hurt."

Adam laughed and lightly tugged her toward the next item on display, a small painting in the modern style.

"Please tell me some kid in kindergarten painted this," Adam said, a little too loudly.

"Shh," she said and swatted him on the upper arm. Just that brief contact raised her awareness of how well formed the arms hiding under that suit jacket were.

He laughed again, and the sound made an unexpected happiness swell inside her. Adam might not be Mr. Perfect Forever, but he was doing a pretty good job of being Mr. Perfect for Tonight. Embarrassing her notwithstanding. Despite the suit, his carefree beach attitude still cloaked him, and it tempted her to adopt it for herself, if only for a little while. His running commentary on all the items on display made her smile grow wider and wider. She wondered what it was like to live a life so free from worry or responsibility.

"Do you always have this much fun?"

"I certainly try." He winked at her, which caused an odd, fluttery sensation to race across her skin.

Good thing he was only a "tonight" guy. He had a way of getting past her defenses and common sense, tempting her to think that things like responsibility and stability maybe didn't matter so much. The suspicion that it was dangerous to spend too much time with him curled its way through her and took root.

"I hear you've been calling David," she said as they perused more items.

"Yeah. Figured the kid might be having a tough time adjusting to the new situation."

"That's kind of you."

He shrugged off her compliment and moved on to the next item, a deep-sea fishing trip.

"How did your conversation with his old man go?"

"Let's just say that he was not happy. I do think I learned a few new curse words."

Adam's jaw clenched, and she got the oddest sensation that he'd now like to punch the guy for saying ugly things to her. He watched her for several seconds before speaking. "You shouldn't have to listen to that."

"It's okay. Job hazard."

When he looked away, she could have kicked herself. Way to go, reminding him that he had a hang-up about women cops.

"Excuse me, son, do you see my earring?" Grace Pierce's voice drew their attention. The chief's mom had her weathered hand on Adam's arm while she scanned the carpeted floor. The distress on her face tugged at Sara's heart. "My Bill gave me those earrings, and I've lost one."

The chief's dad had died of pancreatic cancer two years before. His parents had been married more than fifty years. She still remembered their golden anniversary party the first year she'd been in Horizon Beach.

"Let's see what it looks like," Adam said.

Grace looked up at him, and he gave her one of those heart-melting smiles, then he took a moment to look at the sparkly fall of red and silver in her right ear.

"Okay, we should be able to find that."

To Sara's surprise, he dropped to his hands and knees and started searching the floor. For a moment, all she could do was stare. Then she joined the search, though not on her hands and knees. Other partygoers nearby, having overheard Mrs. Pierce's concern, started looking, as well. A minute passed before Adam found the missing earring.

He stood with it in his palm and presented it to Grace like he was Prince Charming, she was Cinderella and the earring the glass slipper. "It was attempting to hide under the edge of the table."

"Oh, it must have come off when I leaned forward to look at that lovely turquoise necklace." She reached up and patted Adam on the cheek. "Thank you, young man."

"Adam, ma'am."

"Adam." Grace nodded. "I like that name." She glanced over at Sara. "You escorting Sara tonight?"

"I am indeed."

"Then you, dear boy, are envied by many a man in this room."

He caught Sara's gaze as her shock registered. Envied? Because of her?

"I have no doubt," he said.

With another squeeze of his arm, Grace left them alone. Well, as alone as two people can be in a room full of other people.

The band began playing, and Adam extended his hand. Helpless to refuse, even if she'd wanted to, Sara placed her hand in his and allowed him to lead her to the dance floor. For the life of her she couldn't think of a single thing she wanted more than to know what it felt like to be held in his arms.

When he pulled her close to him and placed his strong arm around the small of her back, she feared he'd feel how her heart pounded at his proximity. Frantically, she searched for something reasonably intelligent to say and found a compliment that didn't reveal too much of the excitement bubbling within her.

"That was a nice thing to do for Mrs. Pierce. She and Mr. Pierce were married for a long time."

"He's gone?"

She nodded. "Two years ago. She's the captain's mom."

"Ah. So, maybe I earned you some brownie points with the boss, too."

He fell back on teasing, but something told her

that there was a truly kind place in his heart beneath all that flirtatious, boyish exterior. She'd seen it with David, and now with Mrs. Pierce. That part of her that was always asking questions, digging deeper, wondered why he hid whoever he was behind the persona he projected.

But she'd have to think about that later, when she wasn't being overwhelmed by Adam's nearness, the intoxicating male scent of him, the way she felt purely feminine in his arms. How she wanted to keep dancing cocooned next to him until the sun rose on a new day.

Chapter Seven

Sara owed Ruby and Tana a great debt. She'd tried so hard to get out of tonight's date with Adam. She was glad they hadn't let her.

Even as the last song of the night coasted toward its conclusion, she didn't want the night to end. She couldn't imagine ever feeling so good ever again. Not only did Adam prove a good dancer, but he'd also kept her laughing with his observations of the other people in the room, how they might look in beachwear.

He didn't say anything funny now though. Instead of focusing on his words and dance steps, she became hyperaware of the movements of his body against her. The reined-in strength, how his arms curved around her back, the subtle slide of his suit against her dress, his warmth and clean, male scent.

Oh, God, she had to get home, away from him. She battled the crazy notion that she was halfway to falling for him already.

"I need to be getting home," she said as she pulled back from him with regret.

"Yeah, me, too."

She didn't think he had any pressing reason to get home. Maybe he'd come out of the same lovely fog she'd been in all evening and remembered that she wasn't the type of woman he wanted to be with. Instead of turning into a pumpkin, maybe at midnight she went back to just being a cop to him.

She shook the thoughts away and focused on the light touch of his hand at the small of her back as he guided her out of the ballroom, across the glassed-in hallway and into the parking lot.

"Where are you parked?" he asked.

She pointed in what she hoped was the right direction, though she wasn't positive she could think straight past the whirling of her insides. She didn't want to leave, didn't want to face the fact that she'd never be held in Adam's arms again. Why did it matter so much?

They arrived at her car before she was ready. She closed her eyes, steeled herself before turning toward him. "I had a nice time tonight. Thank you."

"I did, too. I kind of liked being the guy who got all the jealous looks."

"I think you're probably used to that."

"Doesn't mean it wasn't true tonight."

"They're just not used to seeing me in a dress."

He gave her a devilish smile. "Good thing or

they'd never get any work done and Horizon Beach would go to hell."

"Or maybe they were wondering why I'd agreed to go out with a guy who is so incredibly full of it."

He took a step closer. "You really do look beautiful tonight."

She lowered her eyes, feeling so out of her element. "Thank you."

Moments stretched between them, and Sara wondered if he was going to kiss her, if she'd let him. No, that was a really bad idea. Walking away now was hard enough. If she kissed him, she didn't know if she'd be able to continue saying no. If she could convince herself that maybe there was a Mr. Perfect hidden somewhere in Adam Canfield.

She worried that she possessed the same fault her father had—loving someone who didn't love you back.

What was she thinking? She didn't love Adam.

"I better get home, pick up the girls," she said.

He nodded, though she saw something in his eyes, a hesitance that tempted her to believe he didn't want to go any more than she did. With more willpower than it'd taken to get through the police academy, she turned toward her car door as she said, "Good night."

But she couldn't open it, didn't even try.

Why do you always deny yourself? Just because you go out with him doesn't mean you have to marry him. You're still young. Have some fun.

She wanted to scream at the voice in her head, but it won. Her lonely heart won. Sara spun around as Adam was turning to leave. She took two steps, bringing herself next to him, and raised herself to bring her lips to his.

PURE, DEMANDING ADRENALINE surged through Adam when Sara's lips took his. Only a fraction of a second passed before he accepted what she was offering and gave back more of the same. He wrapped his arms around her and lifted her slightly so he could feel all her delicious curves against him.

She tasted like the chocolate-covered strawberries she'd eaten earlier. He'd envied the fruit when he'd watched her lips wrapped around it. Now he caught its flavor and deepened the kiss even more.

Sara moaned into his mouth, and his body reacted as a man's does. He couldn't get close enough to her. He wanted her in bed, now. But some speck of common sense rose up through the haze of lust, told him that pushing her that far would just make her run away. And damn if he was letting her do that. Not when she felt and tasted so good.

When they paused long enough to breathe, he smiled against her soft, wet lips. She didn't feel like a no-nonsense detective now. Maybe he could kiss her well and long enough to make her forget that dangerous job of hers.

"That was unexpected," he said, teasing her as he

liked to do. Something about flustering pretty Sara Greene made life worth living.

She breathed, heavier than normal, against his lips. "Sorry."

"Do not apologize. I liked it."

Sara tried to lower her gaze, but he didn't let her. He lifted her chin, bringing her eyes to his. Then he kissed her again. Gentle, thorough, amazing. She made him feel like all the nerves in his body were hardwired and plugged into an electrical outlet. His skin burned and he wanted nothing more than to rip off his suit, her dress, then press his skin against hers.

Calm down. He broke the kiss but only moved a fraction of an inch back, pushing away all the reasons not to ask the question on the tip of his tongue. "Go to dinner with me tomorrow night."

She moved toward him ever so slightly, as if she couldn't resist, but then she pulled away.

"I can't. I shouldn't be away from the girls two nights in a row."

The mention of the kids should have dampened his desire for her, but it didn't. Odd.

"Fine. But I'm going to keep asking. You're not getting away with just one night."

She opened her mouth to say something but stopped. He imagined the tug-of-war going on inside her head between her practical, responsible self and the part that wanted to tell caution to screw off.

To make his viewpoint on which side should win clear, he leaned forward and kissed her again. "Maybe I can think of something we can do so you can wear those shoes again."

She made a cute little flustered sound before opening her car door. "Good night."

He smiled wide as he stepped back enough for her to slide into her car. His desire thrummed as that sexy red dress rode up her legs before she jerked it back down. Man, he wanted to crawl in that car with her.

He was halfway home before common sense broke through his haze of sexual fantasies. What was he thinking? Going out with her once was one thing. How stupid was he to want to go out with her again, to get closer to her? Hadn't he been down this road before?

He cursed, knew that he should avoid Sara instead of pursuing her. He had a long history of single dates with women. Why should this be any different?

Because none of them had made his body nearly combust when they'd kissed them.

Not even Jessica.

"MUST BE SERIOUS THOUGHTS you're thinking."

Sara jumped at the sound of Captain Pierce's voice on the other side of her desk. Too late, she realized she'd been staring out the window replaying those kisses with Adam for what had to be the millionth time. A flush crept up her neck, prompting her to look down at the paperwork in front of her so she didn't have to face her boss.

"Just brainstorming the Crayton case," she said, thankful she'd been looking at the notes on the robbery only minutes before.

"Any new leads?"

"No, unfortunately."

"Hopefully, someone will slip up and try to sell some of those pieces of jewelry. Speaking of which, wanted to thank you for helping Mom find her earring Saturday night."

"I didn't find it. Adam did."

"Yes, Adam. You two been going out long?"

Sara looked past the captain toward where Keith and Shawn sat at their respective desks. "Did the guys put you up to this?"

The captain looked surprised by her question. "No, why?"

"Oh, nothing. And no, a one-time deal."

"Too bad. I think Mom already has the two of you walking down the aisle."

Sara nearly choked. "Not hardly." Though the image wasn't as farfetched as she'd once thought.

Oh, God, who was she kidding? His kisses made her skin flame and tingle, and he no doubt was awesome in bed. But marriage material? Unlikely.

And yet she continued to think about him and how she'd given in to impulse and kissed him. The memories wrapped her brain in knots as she packed it in and went home for the day. She didn't even notice him sitting on her side deck until she was a few feet away from him.

"Oh, hey," she said, her heartbeat banging away at her eardrums. "What are you doing here?"

"I remembered how much your little one liked pizza, so I thought maybe you'd agree to go out with me if we took the girls to Freddie's."

She didn't manage to hide her surprise. "You want to go out, with all three of us?"

"Well, I want to go out with you. They're just the chaperones."

She searched for a reason to say no, but gave up when it proved too difficult. When was the last time a guy had thrown her like this? "Give me a few minutes to change and go get the girls."

"They're already inside getting ready. Ruby said she thought it was a great idea. I like your neighbor, by the way."

"I'll bet she did," Sara said under her breath as she went in the side door of her house.

She followed the sound of laughter to Lilly's bedroom. Ruby stood behind Lilly, French-braiding her hair.

"We're having pizza, Mommy!"

Sara crossed her arms and eyed Ruby. "So I heard."

Ruby didn't look the least bit sorry when she met her gaze and winked.

FREDDIE'S WAS BUSY as usual. Somehow showing up here with Adam and the girls felt like a bigger step than going to the benefit with him. That was supposed to be one night, one magical night. This continuation of…whatever their relationship was…that wasn't supposed to happen. She felt tense, like she was waiting for him to suddenly realize he wasn't interested anymore and run in the opposite direction.

They found a table near the front, right where everyone coming in the door could see them.

Sara stopped and considered her racing thoughts. Why couldn't she just go with the flow and not analyze everything to death? With a deep breath, she decided to set aside her questions about where this was heading. She knew all dates didn't have to lead to holy matrimony. Maybe if she went out with Adam a few times, she'd lighten up and find the right guy after all without trying so hard.

What if he's across the table from you now?

"So, what kind of pizza does everyone want?" Adam asked.

"Pepperoni," Lilly said with her usual enthusiasm.

"Sausage," Tana said at the same time.

Adam eyed Sara, waiting for her answer. "Whatever, doesn't matter."

He looked at Tana. "What's her favorite kind of pizza?"

"This gross feta-and-spinach thing."

"It's not gross just because you don't like it," Sara said. She met Adam's eyes. "We can go with just a plain cheese. That's something everyone will eat."

"Got it." He headed to the order counter.

As soon as Adam was out of earshot, Tana's smug grin appeared on her face. "He likes you."

Sara sat back in her chair and tried to force all emotion from her expression. "We're acquaintances, friendly. That's all."

Did friendly acquaintances liplock like they had in a hotel parking lot? Did they have steamy daydreams about each other?

Okay, so she was the one daydreaming. Guys didn't obsess like women. She doubted Adam was ignoring his customers at the pier by staring out at the waves and thinking about their kisses.

"Yeah, whatever," Tana said, managing to sound like she had superior knowledge despite her measly thirteen years.

"And from now on, you two and Ruby need to let me handle my own love life, or lack thereof, okay?"

"I like him," Lilly said.

Sara opened her mouth, but Adam spoke first.

"Why, thank you, Miss Lilly." He slid into a chair next to Lilly and put his arm along the back of her chair. "I must say you have good taste in men at an early age."

Lilly giggled and looked over at Sara. The huge smile and glow of happiness on her daughter's face melted any lingering objections Sara had about this group outing. How could anything or anyone who made her daughter that happy be wrong?

But what happened when he wasn't there anymore? Would it break Lilly's little heart?

Sara pushed away the questions as too heavy for the fun, bustling atmosphere of Freddie's. Instead, she focused on the scents of bread and oregano, the rousing Italian music filling the space and the meaningful look in Adam's eyes. Maybe he did think about their kisses after all.

"So, what do you ladies like to do when you have free time?" Adam lavished attention on the girls. If he wanted to maneuver his way into Sara's heart, this was the way to do it. She tried to focus on the reasons why letting him in was a bad idea, but they kept slipping away from her grasp.

"Fly kites," Lilly said.

"Well, this is certainly a good place for that," Adam said.

"Are you a Horizon Beach native?" Sara found herself asking him.

"South Georgia, near Valdosta. Came down here a few years ago to be near the water."

"What did you do before becoming 'pier guy'?" She smiled a little, hoping he'd accept her questioning as gentle teasing, not her compiling facts about him, determining if there was any chance he could be the kind of guy she wanted. No, *needed.* She definitely wanted him, and that could end up being the problem.

The muscles in his face tightened a little. "Was in the army." He directed his attention toward Tana. "What about you? I'm guessing you like music." He nodded toward one of her many band T-shirts. Sara felt old sometimes when she didn't recognize the names. This one said Within Temptation. One of those foreign, symphonic bands with soaring music, Sara guessed.

"You know they're a band?" Tana asked, her face and tone reflecting surprise.

"Yeah. Even saw them in Germany once. Friend of mine dragged me kicking and screaming, but they were actually pretty good."

"Ohmygod, you saw them in concert?"

Thus began a grilling by Tana that would rival that by any detective. She wanted to know what songs they played, what they wore, how awesome was the concert. Of course, Adam, being a guy, had lost a lot of the details.

"It was several years ago," he said. "Sorry."

"That's okay. It's cool that you saw them though. I've never met anyone who has."

"Maybe you can see them when they come to the States sometime." Adam paused and met Sara's gaze. "If your mom says that's okay."

"We'll see." Sara didn't want to commit until she

investigated if the band's concert crowds would be appropriate for a thirteen-year-old.

Freddie himself arrived at the table with not one but four small pizzas. One pepperoni, one sausage, one feta-and-spinach and one supreme.

"You didn't have to get different kinds," Sara said.

"What's the fun of coming to Freddie's if you can't have what you want?"

The way he said it and the devilish twinkle in his eye made Sara realize he wasn't just talking about pizza. She felt like she was in water that was rising fast. Soon, she'd have to decide whether to swim away or allow herself to sink fully.

"What about you, Detective? You a native?"

She shook her head since she was in midbite. After she chewed and swallowed the delicious pizza, she said, "Grew up in Memphis. Came down here for a change of scenery."

"I can relate to that. So, how does a pretty lady like you become a cop?"

"My dad was a police officer. Just following in his footsteps, I guess."

"How does he feel about that?"

"I don't know. He died before I made that decision." How many times had she wondered if he would have approved, needed to know he was proud? She chose to think he'd be honored that she'd chosen the path she had.

She glanced at Adam and a new question formed

in her mind. What would her dad think of Adam? Would he consider him lazy, or would he say she was being too judgmental—just like he had when she'd told him she never wanted to see her mother again?

Chapter Eight

What was he doing here? Why had he thought pursuing Sara and getting more involved with her family had been a good idea? She had kids, for heaven's sake! They were good kids, but kids who required protection and nurturing and all those things he sucked at.

How did a single woman with such a dangerous job even justify having children, ones she could leave orphaned?

But damn if he couldn't seem to help himself. It was like she was some sort of sorceress who attracted him by otherworldly means. And she didn't even seem to be trying.

He did realize over the pizza that he wasn't the only one who had something in his past he'd rather forget. When she'd mentioned her father, he'd seen pain in her eyes. Was it the kind of pain he'd had in his life, or just sorrow that she'd lost a beloved father? He'd bet the latter. Otherwise, it didn't make sense for her to follow in her father's footsteps. He sure hadn't wanted to follow in his dad's.

But it wasn't any of his business. Yes, he had to admit he wanted to continue going out with her, at least a few more times. Kiss her again, maybe more. But he had to draw the line there. Serious was not his bag.

"We'd better be getting home," Sara said as she slipped leftover pizza into a take-home container. "School night. And I bet someone still has homework."

Tana groaned.

Already, Adam's brain raced for when he could see Sara again. Maybe he was coming down with something. A virus that made him act like a lovesick puppy.

He should get home, too, before he started thinking and saying things he didn't need to.

He watched the care Sara took with her daughters, the way the obvious love shone in her eyes, and wondered if he even had the capacity for such caring. If he ever had, in all likelihood the Iraqi sun had burned it out of him.

Adam drove Sara and the girls home. When he stopped in her driveway, she jumped out so quickly he wondered if he made her nervous or if she was having big-time second thoughts about being involved with him at all. Not that they were *involved*. It was only casual, just as he liked it.

Yeah, right. Stop fooling yourself. This woman is different than all the others.

That's what scared him.

He'd swear he could hear his former commander yelling, "Retreat!"

Before he could get out of the car, Sara leaned down and looked in the passenger side window. "Thanks for the pizza. The girls had a nice time."

But had she? Sara didn't say, but she did offer him an entrancing smile before she followed her girls into the house.

He sat there for several long moments, fighting the urge to drive out of Horizon Beach and keep going, before he backed up and headed home. Home to an empty house he had the strangest feeling was going to feel even more empty than normal.

"DID HE KISS YOU good-night?" Tana asked, her big eyes alight, as Sara stepped into the house.

"No." She headed for the refrigerator to put away the leftovers.

Tana followed, undeterred. "Why not?"

Why not, indeed? He hadn't even gotten out of the car.

You didn't give him time. You jumped out of there like a scared rabbit.

"Just because two adults go out doesn't mean they end up kissing."

"Don't you like him?"

"He's fine."

"Are you going out again?"

Sara shoved the pizza in the fridge, closed it and

turned toward Tana. "Why are you pushing this so hard?"

Tana hesitated for a few moments. "Because you seem lonely."

The revelation hit Sara in the gut, and she fumbled for a response. "How can I be lonely with you and Lilly here? And Ruby nearby?"

Tana gave her one of those disgusted teenager looks, the one that said adults didn't have a clue. "It's not the same."

"Honey, grown-up relationships are complicated."

"Don't treat me like a little kid. I'm not stupid."

Sara crossed her arms. "I didn't say you were, but I'll be the one to decide who the right guy is."

Tana shoved her hands into her shorts pockets. "But you don't think it's Adam."

"I don't know. Probably not."

"Why? Because he's not some 'perfect,' boring CPA or something?"

"That's not fair."

"Life's not fair," Tana muttered.

The tinge of bitterness in Tana's words had Sara looking at her more closely. "What's this really about?"

Tana just shrugged. Did she miss her real parents? Or just having a father figure in her life? Sara couldn't help the feeling of failure that washed through her. She did her best to be two parents, but she knew from experience that no one person could truly give a child what she should be getting from two. Her own father had been wonderful, but he hadn't been a loving mother able to teach Sara all the girly things.

"I'll find someone," she said, feeling lame.

"Whatever." Tana headed for her room. Moments later, the door closed, and music came out of her iPod dock speakers.

Lilly appeared in the doorway, her eyes wide and filled with unshed tears. "Why is Tana mad at you?"

Sara lowered herself to Lilly's level. "Oh, honey, she's not. She just doesn't understand some of my decisions." Or lack thereof.

"But she's playing her mad music," Lilly said.

Sara noticed the song playing did sound mad. Should she try to talk to Tana more, get to the core of her upset, or just let her have time to work through whatever was bothering her? An image of herself as a teenager, locked in her room and letting her own version of mad music block out the rest of the world, kept her rooted to the spot.

"Make up," Lilly said, on the verge of letting her tears fall free.

"We will, sweetie pie. Don't worry." Sara leaned forward and kissed her precious baby on the forehead. "Now go on and play in your room for a little bit. Bedtime in an hour."

Lilly hugged her before trudging down the hallway. Sara watched her go, saddened by the fact she wasn't running or skipping like she normally did.

If this was what resulted of her going out with Adam Canfield, tonight had to be the last time. Sure, she wanted a wonderful man to make her family complete, and she had to admit Adam had been wonderful tonight. But no man was worth bringing unhappiness to the family she already had. For the first time, she wondered if the three of them were all there was ever supposed to be. Maybe fate didn't have marriage or love or romance in store for her.

That thought caused a pang in her chest, and she suspected Tana would hate that idea.

Suddenly all kinds of tired, Sara sank onto the floor and leaned against the refrigerator door. Even though Sara could never admit it and make her girls feel like they weren't enough, Tana was right.

She *was* lonely.

And Adam Canfield had made her forget that.

THE ONGOING DEBATE in his head was still being waged like a back-and-forth firefight when Adam pulled in to his own street. He wished he could turn off thoughts about Sara, but he couldn't. He'd tried and failed.

What was it about her that had latched on and refused to let go? Sure, he'd realized at the benefit just how beautiful she was, but he'd dated lots of beautiful women, flirted with them every night at the Beach Bum.

Not recently.

That realization caused his heart to skip a beat. When had he last flirted with someone besides Sara?

He pulled a quick U-turn and headed back through town, looking for the real Adam Canfield. The one who didn't fixate on one woman and neglect his normal flirting routine.

The one who didn't go home before midnight.

The one who didn't feel happy and relaxed around two kids.

Well, all that nonsense was stopping right now. He parked and headed down the beach to the bar.

"Look who decided to show up," Suz said when she spotted him slipping onto his usual perch.

"Dude, where you been?" Zac Parker asked from where he was pouring a beer from the tap.

"I bet I know," Suz said, a self-satisfied smile spreading across her face.

"Sara?" Zac asked.

"Glad to know I'm such a topic of conversation when I'm not here." Adam scanned the bar's patrons, determined to find a lovely woman to occupy his time and his thoughts.

"What?" Suz slid a longneck in front of him. "Just because I tell your best friend you've got the serious hots for someone, suddenly I'm a gossip?"

Adam gripped the cold bottle in his hand. He didn't know what reflected on his face, but Suz backed off.

"So, how's married life treating you?" he asked Zac.

"I highly recommend it," Zac said, the stupid-goofy look of a schmuck in love on his face. "You might want to try it sometime."

Adam cursed in his head. What exactly had Suz told him? "Nah, I'm more the play-the-field type." As if to prove his point to them, and himself, he met the eyes of a pretty brunette three tables away. "No commitments for me."

He slipped off the stool and headed for the brunette. As he grew closer, he shoved away images of Sara looking at him from across the table at Freddie's, of her in that sexy red dress. When he realized the girl in front of him must be a decade younger than he was, Suz's previous comment about him becoming a dirty old man came back to haunt him.

What the hell was happening to him? He'd never even paused before.

He made an effort. He really did. But by the time fifteen minutes had passed with Leila and her friends, all college students from Panama City, he had to get away. It didn't feel right, and he hated that he could feel his carefree life slipping away.

Adam excused himself, left his unfinished beer on the bar and walked out without a word to Suz or Zac. Let them think what they would. He wasn't in the mood to talk to anyone. As he drove home, he was now thankful an empty house awaited him. No one should be around him when he was in a foul temper.

Damn David Taylor anyway. Adam's life would be just fine if David hadn't run away from home. If he hadn't, Sara Greene would have remained only someone he saw in passing around town. He wouldn't be all twisted up in knots about her.

Adam pulled in to his driveway and cut the engine, then slammed the heel of his hand against the steering wheel. How much of an ass was he for wishing David hadn't run away when the kid had been in danger?

God, if Sara was smart she'd tell him to take a hike. She deserved someone better.

AFTER SEEING TANA OFF to school and leaving Lilly with Ruby the next morning, Sara went for a run on the beach and deliberately headed toward the pier. She'd lain awake until nearly 2:00 a.m. thinking about Adam and how he'd turned her world upside down in such a short time. If Ruby, Tana and Lilly all liked him, could they all be wrong? Had Ruby been right that there was no such thing as Mr. Perfect?

As her running shoes beat against the packed sand at the edge of the water, she remembered how sad both of the girls had looked at breakfast. For some reason, they'd grown fond of Adam very quickly, and she wondered if maybe they saw things more clearly than she did. Were kids' instincts about people better than those of adults because they didn't overanalyze

everything so darn much? Was fate trying to tell her
something through those sad faces? Should she stop
fighting it and give Adam a real chance? If he wanted
it, that was.

She swallowed the nervousness that she'd come
to this decision too late, that his not getting out of
the car last night meant that sometime over pizza
he'd decided two dates with her was enough.

Well, she'd find out soon. The pier was only a
hotel length away.

Only he wasn't there.

An older guy sporting a Hawaiian shirt and a bit
of a paunch sat in Adam's spot and blinked back at
her. "You wanting to go out on the pier?"

"Uh, no. I thought Adam was working this morning."

"Called in sick." The guy sounded annoyed, like
Adam's call had torpedoed his plan to sleep all day.

"Oh. Well, thanks."

Feeling awkward, she turned and hurried off the
pier. Something told her the guy was watching her
retreat, so she jogged in the other direction, up past
the Beach Bum, over the dunes, through the parking
lot back to the sidewalk along the street.

She refused to read meaning into the fact that
Adam hadn't been at the pier. He'd said he was sick.
Maybe fate wasn't trying to tell her something in
code at every turn. Deciding to take the explanation
at face value, she jogged toward home.

Once there, she showered and got ready for work. Her caretaker instincts nearly got the best of her when she opened the cabinet to grab a bag of pretzels to take with her and she spotted the cans of chicken noodle soup. Those helped when you felt bad, right?

With a groan, she shut the cabinet door. She did *not* know Adam well enough to go to his house bearing chicken noodle soup for what ailed him. She shouldn't even know he was sick.

She determined not to try so hard, not to let this fixation take over. Work beckoned as a way to fill her thoughts with other things, so she hurried to the station.

Unfortunately, what waited for her there made her wish she could go back to conflicting thoughts about Adam Canfield. They would have been less disturbing.

Chapter Nine

Murder redirected Sara's main focus back to her job. It took two days to figure out who had killed eighty-seven-year-old Betsy Turnbow in her little house at the edge of the county and another to find her grandson where he was hiding out in Crestview. Sara felt a decade older when she came home after his arrest. She wondered why she was always surprised when some new ugliness passed through her jurisdiction.

When she got home and pulled in to the driveway, she spotted Tana chasing Lilly with the spraying garden hose, both of them laughing. Ruby sat on the porch, knitting needles in hand and a wide smile on her face.

For the first time, she wondered if a different job choice would have been wiser if she wanted a family. A job that wasn't so steeped in the worst part of humanity.

The sorrow of what she'd seen the past couple of days prodded her to back out of the drive and not contaminate the happy scene before her, but she didn't. As she sat, marrow-weary, someone parked behind her. A couple of fatigued moments passed before she realized it was Adam. Even with the extra jolt of adrenaline seeing him gave her, it still proved a colossal effort to drag herself from her car.

"Hey," he said as he rounded the back of his car and opened the trunk.

"Hey. I didn't expect to see you here."

He pulled a bright pink-and-purple butterfly kite from the trunk. "I saw this at the kite shop downtown. I thought Lilly might like it."

For a brief moment, an air of awkwardness enveloped him. He glanced at the kite as if he couldn't believe he'd bought it.

"Hope you don't mind," he said as he met her gaze again.

She stared for a moment, trying to figure him out, but she honestly didn't see an ulterior motive in his eyes. Something shifted inside of her, something that made her want to cry at his thoughtful gesture. "No, of course not. She'll love it."

The nearly overwhelming desire to walk into his arms, to soak in the fact that there was indeed goodness in the world, made her cross her arms and look toward where the girls came running from the opposite direction.

Lilly stopped and stared at the kite. Her mouth formed an O of wonder. "It's bootiful," she said, her words filled with awe.

Adam took a few steps. "I'm glad you like it because it's for you."

Lilly looked at Sara for confirmation, for permission. The moment Sara nodded that the wonder-kite was indeed hers, Lilly sprinted forward with a squeal of glee.

"Can we go fly it, Mommy? Please!" Lilly's little body wasn't big enough to contain all the excitement flowing from her.

Sara didn't care how tired or drained she was, she wasn't going to deny her daughter's fondest wish—to fly her new kite.

"Sure, sweetie. Just let me change, and we'll head over to the beach."

"Will you come, too?" Lilly asked Adam, an uncharacteristic shyness in her voice.

Adam met Sara's eyes. "If your mom doesn't mind."

"No, it's fine." An attack of nerves sent Sara fleeing for the house.

When she reached her room, she sank onto the side of the bed. She expected someone to follow her inside, but no one did. Instead, they stayed outside with Adam. She glanced at her reflection in the mirror. Big mistake. Dark half-moons under her eyes and the lines of fatigue stared back at her. It was a wonder Adam hadn't fled at the mere sight of her.

But he hadn't.

He'd brought a kite to her daughter—and a smile of purest joy to her face.

Sara rose and made quick work of washing her face, brushing her hair and pulling it into a fresh ponytail, and changing into a yellow tee and white shorts. It wasn't a shower or twelve hours of uninterrupted sleep, but at least she felt marginally better. She could have put on makeup to camouflage the dark circles and remnants of the bruise on her cheek, but she decided if this...whatever it was...with Adam had the remotest hope of working, he had to see the real her. The one who sometimes worked long hours and came home spent and a little worse for wear. At least she'd know the truth of his supposed interest.

When she made her way back outside, she found both of the girls at the edge of the lawn talking to Adam. She watched them, wondering if that could become a forever type of image.

"Give him a chance," Ruby said as she stepped up beside her.

Sara watched for a moment more, trying to keep herself from judging Adam against the model of perfection she'd had in her mind for years. "I am."

After tearing the girls away from Adam long enough to get them buckled into the car, Sara glanced at Adam. "We'll follow you."

The drive to the nearest public beach access only took five minutes, but Sara's heart thumped in anticipation the entire way there. She barely heard anything the girls said.

Once they reached the beach, her concerns and anticipation stepped aside as her mothering instinct took over. She retrieved the new kite from the trunk and helped Lilly get it airborne.

"Oh, Mommy, look! The butterfly's flying," Lilly said as she ran as fast as her little legs would carry her.

Sara hugged herself and watched as Tana took her spot and helped keep her little sister's new toy flying high. The steady sea breeze made the pink and green streamers at the base of the kite dance in the air.

"She seems to like it," Adam said next to her.

"Yeah." She looked over at him, trying to figure out what other hidden parts of Adam Canfield lay beneath his flirtatious and supposedly carefree exterior. "Thank you."

He glanced at her and smiled. "You sound surprised."

"Do I?"

He laughed a little. "Not that I blame you. Can't say I thought I'd be buying a kite today when I got up."

"Why did you? Buy a kite." Had it simply been a ploy to get into her good graces? Something told her no, probably the honesty in his expression when he'd said he'd been as surprised by his act as she was.

Adam slipped his hands into his pockets and watched the girls laughing as they ran with the kite, making it snap against the salty wind. He shrugged. "Don't know. I saw it and thought of Lilly. They just seemed to go together."

She returned her gaze to her daughters, and her heart swelled. This man, the one she'd deemed totally inappropriate for their lives, had made two girls laugh and smile so wide their cheeks must surely hurt.

"Want some lemonade?" he asked.

A moment passed before Sara pulled herself out of the heady realization that Adam was carving a place for himself not only in the girls' hearts, but also in her own. Honestly, it scared her, but she felt powerless to stop it. She looked in his direction and noticed he was indicating the frozen lemonade stand down the beach.

"Sure. Sounds good."

She watched as he walked toward the stand, and her heart performed a series of flips any gymnast would envy.

"You like him," Tana said in a singsongy, teasing voice as she came close. "I knew it."

"Okay, fine, I like him. Are you happy?"

Tana's smile grew even wider. "Why, yes, I am."

Sara laughed and pulled Tana next to her, tickled her until she squealed and wriggled free. Tana dropped to the sand and sat back on her heels a couple of feet away.

"He's nice. Cooler than other guys you've gone out with."

"Hey."

Tana gave a matter-of-fact shrug. "It's the truth."

Sara rolled her eyes and turned her attention to Lilly's kite-flying efforts.

"Are you going to go out with him again?" Tana asked.

Sara lowered her gaze to the sand. "I don't know, maybe."

"You should. You two look good together."

Sara raised her eyebrow. "And you have so much experience matchmaking."

"Just common sense. Some people look good together. Some don't."

"Looking good together isn't the most important thing."

"Doesn't hurt."

Sara spotted Adam returning with the lemonades. No, it certainly didn't hurt.

"You've got it bad," Tana said before she jumped to her feet and ran back toward Lilly, leaving Sara to admit to herself that her oldest might be right.

The moment she acknowledged it, a flood of yearning washed through her. If she and Adam were alone, she wasn't the least bit sure she wouldn't push him back in the sand and kiss him senseless.

"Thanks," she said when he handed her the icy lemonade. She took a long drink, enjoyed the tartness on her tongue and the cool feel of the ice sliding down her throat. "That's just what the doctor ordered."

"Tough day?" he asked as he settled beside her in the sand.

She nodded.

"The Turnbow case?" He sounded hesitant, as if he wasn't sure he really wanted to ask the question.

"Yeah." She didn't even try to disguise the fatigue and sorrow she'd carted home with her.

"Makes you wonder how humanity has lasted this long when we go around killing each other, doesn't it?"

Something in the way he said it, like he was tapping an unthinkable memory, made Sara look at him, examine his strong, attractive profile. He turned, locked his eyes with hers.

"What makes you say that?" Did her voice sound breathy, or was that only in her head?

He broke eye contact and turned his attention to the waves rolling onto the edge of the shore. "Just seems like that's all that's on the news anymore."

She suspected there was more to his observation, but she didn't question him. Instead, she took another drink of her lemonade and focused all her thoughts on the cold, refreshing taste. She let the simple pleasure of drinking lemonade on the beach with a good-looking man at her side while her daughters enjoyed flying a kite replace all the ugliness of the past couple of days.

"So, you going to let me take you out sometime, without the girls tagging along?" He asked it with that familiar flirtatious tone in his voice.

She smiled. "I don't know. Maybe."

"Well, that's better than a no," he said, then laughed as the kite fell right on top of Lilly's head.

HE WAS TEMPTING FATE, but Adam didn't care. From the moment Sara Greene had dived off that pier after him, his brain hadn't been functioning properly anyway. To his surprise, she showed up at the Beach Bum after work the day following the girls' kite-flying excursion. They did nothing more than sit and have a drink together, but it was nice and easy. For the first time, he thought back to how much work all the flirting had been. He'd never realized it, especially since he'd tried to work as little as possible.

The next day, they met for lunch. By the end of the meal, he'd captured her hand atop the table. And she didn't seem to mind.

When the day after that she invited him to a cookout at her house, he had to admit the woman had invaded not only nearly all his thoughts, but also his very bloodstream. That part of himself that had sworn never to get serious about a woman again berated him for allowing this to go so far, but he sent those thoughts back into the dark corners of his mind. Hard to do when the Turnbow case had been all over the news and he'd suspected she'd helped to solve it.

Being with Sara gave him a sense of happiness he hadn't felt in a long time. Not since those hot, dusty but intoxicating days with Jessica.

That thought caused him to hit the brakes on his car, eliciting a lot of horn honking behind him. He pulled in to a parking lot, realized he'd broken out in a cold sweat. He couldn't do this, not again. God, what had he been thinking?

"Hey, what are you doing here?"

Adam started, jerked out of those faraway memories by Zac's voice. His best friend stood outside the car, a bouquet of multicolored flowers in his hand. A couple of seconds ticked by before he realized he'd pulled into the parking area for Hearts and Flowers Florist.

Darn small town. Ran into people you knew everywhere you went, and usually when you didn't want to.

"Are you okay?" Zac leaned over, took a closer look.

Adam wanted to jerk the car into gear and race from the parking lot, drive full out until he escaped the memories that refused to let him find any peace.

That's when he realized he hadn't dreamed of Jessica in…not since the night before the kite flying on the beach. When had he ever gone that long without some form of the dream torturing him?

He nodded. "I thought the car was overheating, but the light just went off." The excuse sounded lame, but it was the best he could do with his jumbled-up brain.

"Uh-huh." Zac sounded like he knew exactly what was bugging Adam.

Not likely since Adam hadn't uttered a word

about Jessica, about the dreams, about the real reason he'd left the army. Since he and Zac had known each other, all Adam had been was the carefree beach bum, the incurable flirt.

The hollowness of the past few years slammed into him, which didn't make any sense. That's what he wanted, right? To not have to be responsible for anything or anyone, to simply float through life until he came to the end of it.

Images of David and Sara filtered through his mind. Damn if he wasn't reverting back to the person he'd been before that bomb had scarred him in more ways than were visible.

"I gotta go." Adam didn't offer any explanations. Maybe he'd explain someday, maybe not. Right now, he just had to get away from Zac and his questions, from that cursed glow of newlywed bliss.

He ignored the guilt that gnawed at him more the farther away from Sara's house he drove. He might be a bit of a dog when it came to women, but he'd never stood one up. And worse, he felt like he was standing up Tana and Lilly, too.

It wasn't his fault they'd latched on to him.

No, he'd just taken them out for pizza, bought Lilly a kite, bought chocolate from Tana for her art club's fundraiser.

Adam gritted his teeth as he nearly took out his mailbox while swerving into his driveway. His neighbors would likely think he was drunk, but he didn't care. After he got out of the car, he slammed the door so hard he wouldn't have been surprised if it had come flying out the other side of the car. The door to the house got the same type of abuse. Once inside, however, Adam just stood in the middle of the living room, wondering what he could possibly do to make himself feel better about ditching on Sara's cookout without a word.

Nothing. You deserve to suffer.

Yeah, that was new.

He knew only one way to get through the night. Luckily, he'd stocked up on beer just the day before. He feared it was going to take a good quantity to get Sara Greene out of his head.

Cold one in hand, he plunked down on the couch and flicked on the TV, channel surfed until he found one of the *Terminator* movies. Good, he was in the mood for some futuristic shooting and blowing up stuff.

When the phone rang some time later, he ignored it. At least he tried to. But the stupid thing kept ringing. He'd jerk the cord out of the wall, but that would require him to move. When the answering machine clicked on, he wished he'd made the effort.

Tana's voice invaded his home, the bubble of numbness he was trying hard to create. "Hey, thought you might have forgotten the time for the cookout. We're all here, food's done, see ya."

No, she wouldn't.

Chapter Ten

Adam was about as friendly as a snake that had been poked with a stick. All the next day, it took way more effort than he liked to expend to not bite off the heads of everyone who came to the pier. He skipped his normal visit to the Beach Bum altogether and dreaded the questions that would arouse.

The bad mood accompanied him home for a second night and refused to unstick itself from him or let him rest. Though he was dog-tired, after a couple of hours of subpar sleep, he found himself roaming the house. He didn't turn on the lights, didn't want to illuminate the person he'd become.

A guy who ditched a nice woman without an explanation.

A man who refused to let go of the past.

One who was so damned scared of caring for someone again that he refused to acknowledge it was happening.

He dropped to the couch and sat staring at nothing in particular, his mind whirling.

Was it possible for him to set aside what had happened in Iraq and attempt an actual relationship with Sara? Part of his mind screamed yes, but it was the part dying to be with her right this very minute. Should he pay attention to it or to the part that told him to stay away, to protect himself?

He let his head drop back against the top of the couch and stared at the ceiling. For once, he wished someone or something would tell him what to do—because he sure didn't know himself.

He woke up just before daybreak with a horrible crick in his neck. Served him right. As he sat and let sleep ebb, he realized that the idea of getting serious about Sara didn't seem as bad this morning as it had the night before. He kept waiting for his common sense to smack him upside the head, but it didn't. Not when he trudged to the bathroom. Not as he showered and dressed. Not as he walked out into the dawn of another day.

By the time he drove in to the parking lot of the Coffee Cottage, his mood lightened. He began to think of all the years of keeping his distance as a sentence that had to be paid, and maybe it was finally over. He was so stunned that he didn't even notice Ruby until he almost ran into her. She stood in line staring at her phone. When she looked up and noticed him, he didn't get a warm, fuzzy feeling.

At a loss for what to say, he glanced at the phone in her hands. "Twittering again?"

She didn't smile. "Doubt you'd like what I'm saying."

He let out a long sigh. "That I'm a big jerk."

"Enormous."

What was he supposed to say to that? She was right.

"You know, I told Sara to give you a chance. Now I feel like a fool."

"I didn't mean to hurt her." He was surprised anyone would care enough about him to even make that scenario possible.

"She wasn't the only one."

He could still hear Tana's voice on his answering machine even though he'd erased the message.

"Those girls see something in you. They've never latched on to someone Sara's dated before."

"They shouldn't have."

"Yeah, well, they did. Get over it." Ruby moved to the front of the line and ordered her coffee before turning toward him again. "Despite your imitation of a weasel the other day, I still think there's hope for you, too. Sara, however, is going to take more convincing."

Ruby paid, grabbed her coffee cup and left without another word. Adam was left with the feeling that she wanted him to do that convincing.

Now to figure out how.

"THAT SHOULD DO IT for now, Mr. Wainwright," Sara said as she closed her notebook. "We'll contact you if we have any more questions or if we learn anything."

Mr. Wainwright, who owned a pawnshop on the outskirts of town and who'd been robbed to the tune of several thousand dollars, nodded and turned to start cleaning up the mess the burglars had left behind.

Sara stepped outside into the bright sunlight and shaded her eyes. She faltered when she saw Adam walking toward her from where her car was parked. What was he doing here?

And she had about five seconds to decide how she was going to react to him after he was a no-show at her cookout. Act like nothing had happened, thus not letting him know how much it had hurt her? Or giving him a piece of her mind, thus making her stupid feelings obvious?

"Hey," he said as he reached her. "The guys at the station said I could find you here."

"Oh." Nonchalance, that sounded good.

He shifted from one foot to the other. "Listen, I'm just going to say it. I'm an idiot and an ass on top of that."

"Very self-observant of you." She started walking toward her car, and he fell into step beside her.

"I'm sorry I bailed on the cookout and didn't call."

She shrugged. "No problem."

He wrapped his hand around her wrist and stopped walking, forcing her to stop, too.

"I'm not going to make excuses, but I am sorry if...I hurt anyone." He said the last with an uncertain tone, like he wasn't sure he should even utter the words.

"It's a free country, Adam. You can come and go as you like." It wasn't as if she hadn't known he'd bail at some point anyway. She'd just let her herself ignore that fact.

"Let me make it up to you," he said.

"Not necessary."

"Okay. Then let me take you out tonight just because I want to."

That was all she could stand. She turned fully toward him. "You don't owe me anything. I know you're a play-the-field guy. Everyone knows that. No hard feelings."

He caught her gaze and held it. "Right now, I don't want to go out with someone else. I want to go out with you."

No matter how hard she tried to prevent it, those words soaked into her, made hope flare to life again. She was an idiot for even considering continuing down this road. She needed to get out now while she could.

"Adam—"

"I'm just going to keep asking until you say yes, so you might as well cave now."

He sounded so much like his flirty, fun self that a

laugh escaped her despite the warning alarms screaming against her eardrums.

She slipped her wrist out of his hand and crossed her arms. "What do you have in mind?"

"It's a surprise," he said. "Meaning, of course, that I don't know yet."

She laughed and shook her head.

"Just be ready at seven," he said.

With a big smile, he turned and left before she could change her mind, come back to her senses.

She wouldn't give him the satisfaction of watching him leave, so she slipped into the driver's seat of her car and sat, staring in the opposite direction. She was probably a fool for not walking away now while the hurt was still manageable, but she couldn't.

She'd just deal with whatever pain there would be when the time came.

SARA FUMBLED THROUGH her jewelry box, trying to find something to go with her blue-and-white sundress. Nerves made her dump half of the contents onto the top of her dresser. What was wrong with her? She'd been out with Adam before, had spent time with him on other occasions.

But not after she'd thought he'd left her life only to return again with apologies and pleas for another chance.

Tonight felt different, like they were taking a bigger step.

"You sure about this?" Tana asked from the open doorway.

"It's just a date. I'm going in with my eyes wide open. Besides, I thought you liked Adam."

"That was before he pulled the 'disappearing dude' act."

Sara stopped her search for the right jewelry and looked at Tana. "He apologized, and I'm giving him the benefit of the doubt. You know I believe people deserve second chances."

"But not thirds?"

"Depends, but probably not."

"Fine, he gets another chance. Here." Tana extended a wrapped gift toward Sara.

"What's this?" The girls had already given her their birthday gifts that morning over breakfast.

"Something I thought you could wear tonight. It didn't arrive until today."

Sara took the package wrapped in shiny blue paper very like the blue swirls in her dress. When she opened the box inside, a necklace and earrings that looked like white daisies sat on a bed of cotton.

"Oh, Tana, these are so pretty. Where did you get them?"

"The wonders of eBay."

Sara met her daughter's eyes, questioning.

"Don't worry. I didn't use your credit card. I made some money drawing stuff for people at school, and I gave it to Ruby. She used her credit card to order it."

Sara ran her fingertips over the large daisy on the necklace. "Thank you. I love them."

Sara slipped the earrings into her ears and allowed Tana to help fasten the necklace.

"Adam's going to swallow his tongue," Tana said as she stepped back and looked at Sara's ensemble.

"Tana," Sara gently scolded.

"Well, he is." Something in the way she said those words sounded determined, like a plea to the universe. Tana grew quiet, more serious. "I want you to be happy."

"I am happy."

"Yeah, I know. You tell us that all the time, like you think we're going to break if you don't remind us on a daily basis."

Shock prevented Sara from speaking. Is that what she'd communicated to her daughters?

"It's okay. Lilly and I know you love us, and we love you. But it's not the same as romance, is it?"

Sara looked down at her hands in her lap and had to admit the truth. "No. But I've never been really good at romance."

"Because of your parents?"

Sara's gaze went to Tana's. "Did Ruby say something to you?"

"No." Tana shrugged. "I just figured things out. Not hard to figure out your obsession with finding us the perfect dad must have something to do with yours."

Sara shook her head back and forth slowly. "You're like a wise old woman in a teenager's body."

"What did he do?"

Sara took a deep breath, realized that Tana was old enough to hear and maybe understand. "It wasn't my dad. He was great. My mom left us when I was young. Dad did the best he could filling the gap."

"But he wasn't a mom."

Sara gave Tana a sad smile. "No. I guess that's why I'm so determined to be a good mom."

"And why you watch all those old shows about perfect families?"

"Maybe. Mainly, it's because those are the shows I watched with my dad. They're comfort viewing."

"Why did your mom leave?"

"I don't know really." Although her dad had always suspected there was another man in the picture.

Tana made a disgusted sound. "Does everyone have screwed-up parents?"

"It seems that way, doesn't it? But there are good ones, too. That's important to remember." She turned toward Tana. "You, Lilly, me—we've all been through situations where parents let us down. That's why I've wanted so much to make our family happy and full of love."

"We're happy. But this dad stuff—if he stops being a jerk, I'd rather have Adam than one of those dudes on the shows you watch. Nobody's that perfect. And if they were, I couldn't stand them." Tana wrinkled her nose, which made Sara laugh.

"Point taken."

The sound of a car arriving in the driveway made Sara's heart rate kick up.

Tana, who was closer to the window, looked outside. "Your *just-a-date* is here."

Sara rolled her eyes at Tana as she headed for the door into the hall. She stopped and turned back toward her oldest. "You know that even Adam might not work out, right? I don't want you to get your hopes up too high."

"Whatever you say," Tana said with a smug, know-it-all look on her face. She might as well have said she did, indeed, think Adam was the one for Sara.

As Sara headed out to meet Adam, she couldn't deny she hoped Tana was right.

GIDDINESS MADE IT impossible for Sara to stop smiling. The feel of Adam's gentle touch at the small of her back as they weaved their way among the blankets already spread across the grass of Lakeview Park made her skin tingle. He'd surprised her by his choice of movie night in the park for their date, but she had to admit he'd scored big romantic points for it.

They found a spot near the edge of the grassy area next to a palm tree. Adam spread their blanket out while she held the picnic basket he'd brought along but hadn't let her peek into.

Her stomach growled.

Adam grinned. "Glad to know you're hungry."

Sara's face flushed. "Busy day. Didn't have time to eat much." Okay, so she'd been way more nervous than she should have been after seeing him and unable to eat more than a few bites here and there, but he didn't need to know that.

"Busy, huh?" Drat the man for sounding like he knew the truth behind her fib.

They settled on the blanket, and Sara finally got to see what was inside the wicker basket. Adam pulled out minisandwiches of several different types, chopped vegetables with dip, chilled bottled water and brownies.

"You make this?"

"You'd better hope not," he said. "I'm the king of takeout."

"Oh, good to know I won't get food poisoning."

They ate as the movie screen started to flicker. When the title of the movie came up, she nearly choked on a tiny chicken salad sandwich. *The Perfect Man* starring Heather Locklear as a single mom and Hilary Duff as the teenage daughter trying to find her mom the perfect guy. Either Tana could pull strings with the tourism commission, or fate had an enormous sense of humor.

She'd seen the movie before, but watching it beneath the stars with Adam, nibbling on picnic food, smelling the incoming sea breeze—it was easily the best birthday she'd ever had.

When they'd finished their sandwiches and veggies, Adam pulled something else from the recesses of the picnic basket. As she watched, he placed a candle in the top of one of the brownies, lit it and held it out to her.

"Happy birthday."

"How did you know?"

"I have my ways."

"I bet your 'way' happens to have white hair and live across the street from me."

As she stared at the brownie, her heart swelled at the simple and thoughtful gesture. She leaned forward and kissed him lightly on the lips, only pulling back when she realized the flame was dangerously close to the front of her dress.

"Ack, I'm about to set myself on fire." She lowered her head and blew out the candle, wishing, unrealistically, that this night would never end.

As they ate their brownies, Adam wrapped his arm around her and guided her to his side. He leaned against the trunk of the palm tree, and she cuddled up next to him, soaked up his delicious warmth as they watched the movie. When Chris Noth extended a rose and said, "There is such a thing as perfect, and it's out there," Sara truly felt for the first time that she had already found it.

As if he knew what she was thinking, Adam kissed the top of her head, then shifted so he could kiss her temple. A moment more and his lips were on hers. Warm, soft yet firm, and so very nice. Sara let herself sink fully into the kiss, her birthday present to herself.

When the kiss ended, he smiled down at her and said, "Happy birthday."

She smiled back. "You said that already."

"What, there's a limit?"

"No, I guess not."

"Good, because I think I might have a few more birthday wishes in me."

Sara's heart rate kicked up again at his words. All birthdays should be this great.

As the credits of the movie started to roll and the people around them began folding blankets, Adam whispered in her ear. "You ready to get out of here?"

No, she wasn't. She didn't want to go home, didn't want this night to come to a close. Some need she'd been ignoring for a long time roared to life within her. Maybe the night didn't have to end just yet.

Her nerves sparked like electricity gone wild as they gathered their things and walked back to his car. When he opened her door for her, she swallowed the nervousness threatening to overtake her and turned to face him.

"This is the best birthday I've had in a long time," she said.

He smiled that sexy, flirty smile of his. "Be careful, you might make my ego go supersize."

"It's a chance I'm willing to take."

His expression changed. He didn't really look serious, but his playfulness stepped aside and showed a bit more of the man beneath.

"I'm glad. I had a good time, too." He lowered his lips to hers again, this time in a kiss so tender it caused her heart to expand and reach for him.

All of her senses were heightened. She felt every nuance of the kiss, every movement of Adam's hands on her back, every thumping heartbeat in her chest. When they parted for air, she tamped down her normal caution.

"Would you like to come back to my place for some birthday cake?"

She wanted much more than to feed him cake and he probably knew it. But no matter how daring she tried to be, she wasn't the type of woman to come right out and invite him home for sex. It was hard enough to even accept that she was willing to have sex with him, knowing that despite how perfect he'd felt tonight he might not be the best man for her.

Why wasn't he?

The question stopped her, made her examine who Adam Canfield was outside of a guy who flirted with tremendous regularity and who eschewed responsibility as if it was the Ebola virus.

He was a guy who bought her daughter a kite just

because he thought she'd like it. He was a guy who gave her the most romantic birthday of her life. Maybe Ruby and Tana were right. Maybe her idea of perfect wasn't realistic. Maybe perfect was holding her in his arms right now.

With a final kiss, he ushered her into the car. But as soon as he got in and pulled out of the lot, he reached across and wrapped her hand in his. Warmth curled its way up her arm and throughout her body, the kind of warmth that made the world take on a shiny new glow.

Her nervousness threatened to dim the glow, however, when they reached her driveway. Was she making a mistake?

Stop second-guessing yourself.

She kept that mantra running through her mind as she got out of the car, unlocked the front door and led him to the kitchen. She hadn't been in the kitchen more than fifteen seconds when her phone signaled she had a text message. Who would be texting her this late? If it was Tana, she was so grounded.

But it was from Ruby. *Girls are asleep. Just get them in the morning.*

Hmm. Sara only half believed her neighbor's claim. She had a sneaky suspicion Ruby had seen Adam come inside with her and wanted him to spend the night. She didn't know whether to scold Ruby or thank her.

She glanced up and met Adam's eyes, eyes that

held desire in them. If they delivered on the unspoken promise, she'd be forced to thank Ruby in the morning.

She smiled as she turned toward the fridge to retrieve the cake. When she had her back to him, she texted a response. *OK.*

As she started to open the refrigerator, Adam came up behind her and wrapped his arms around her waist. His breath warm next to her ear, he whispered, "I'm not hungry for cake."

Chapter Eleven

Sara held her breath, aware this was her point of no return. The thought of tumbling into bed with Adam flushed her skin and sent yearning surging through her.

"Me neither," she said, then turned toward this man who kept surprising her.

His mouth captured hers the moment she faced him, hungrier this time. He groaned as his hands slid up her back and pulled her closer—close enough that she felt the physical effect she was having on him.

That knowledge fueled her own passion, and she deepened the kiss even more. Somehow, they moved away from the fridge and she kicked it closed with half a thought and started leading him, their mouths still tasting each other, down the hall toward her room.

Adam's hands, strong hands with long fingers, slid up her neck and into her hair, urging her mouth closer to his own.

A sense of urgency followed them, like they were

both determined to feel the other but afraid the other would back out before skin met skin. Desire licked at Sara like bright, intoxicating flames, waiting for her consent to burst into a full conflagration.

"You're sure?" Adam rasped as if it took all his willpower to ask the question.

The fact he would ask when he was so heavily aroused knocked aside whatever lingering doubt might have been lurking in Sara's mind. She wasn't sure she could speak, so instead she took a step away and, before she could think herself into backing out, lifted her dress over her head.

When she tossed it aside, she noticed Adam staring. Self-consciousness assaulted her as she looked down at herself.

"What?"

Adam closed the distance between them and ran his fingertips over the part of her breast exposed above her bra. "You're beautiful. And I want you, now."

Sara knew the feeling. She tugged his shirt from the waistband of his jeans. "Then you're going to need to get rid of this." When he whipped off the shirt and flung it aside, she ran the tip of her index finger along the inside of the top of his jeans. "And these."

He leaned forward. "Why don't you help me?"

Her nerves crackled as she reached for the button on his jeans and worked it loose. The nervousness made her hesitate, but then Adam's hands were there, helping her lower his zipper so slowly she thought

she might scream. Before the jeans came off, however, Adam pulled her close and kissed her again.
First her lips, then her cheek, moving to the lobe of
her ear and trailing down her neck to the swell of her
breasts.

Sara's hands went to the back of Adam's head,
her fingers snaking through his hair, pressing him
closer. Those wonderful hands of his slid under her
bra and flicked open the clasp. Then they moved
down to the waistband of her panties, and started
sliding them down as he captured one of her breasts
in his warm, wet mouth.

Sara's body spasmed with pleasure and demanded
more. So much more. She shoved her hands inside
his jeans, and he got the message. A few more heated
moments and they were both naked and falling back
onto the bed, a tangle of limbs and crazy desire.
Sara's ability to think was so occupied with physical
sensation that she barely recognized the sound of a
foil wrapper ripping before Adam was there, above
her, looking down at her in the half dark.

"This is what you want?" he asked, looking like
he might die if she said no.

Something about the expression on his face, a
sort of unexpected hopefulness, had her thinking that
he didn't always ask this before making love to a
woman. She tried not to examine the thought too
closely, to assign it too much meaning.

"Yes," she said and captured his mouth for another

kiss. She couldn't get enough of those kisses, like they were some exotic delicacy she was helpless to resist.

Even though they'd been touching a lot tonight, Sara was totally unprepared for the feel of Adam's body next to hers with nothing between them. If she'd known it would make her feel more alive than she'd felt in her entire life, she would have caved the first time he'd flirted with her. So she was glad she hadn't known, because now she'd discovered there was more to him than what he often showed the world around him.

He was a man to whom she could lose her heart if she wasn't careful.

If she hadn't already.

With Adam's next movement, Sara's thoughts fragmented like lovely shattered glass into single impressions. The feel of Adam's back muscles moving under her hands. The warmth of his breath as it moved across her skin. The sounds of pleasure coming from them both. And finally the tightening of her own muscles, as well as Adam's entire body, as they reached the peak of their lovemaking.

Adam sank beside her, his mouth next to the crook of her neck. "That...was..." He sounded like he could barely breathe, and that made Sara smile as she supplied a word to finish his sentence.

"Awesome."

"Yeah."

She ran her hand over his sweat-slickened back,

loving the feel of those sinewy muscles. How could a guy who sat on a pier or a bar stool all the time stay in such good shape? Did he have a gym at home? Did he run? Both things seemed at odds with what she knew about him, but then hadn't she been discovering he was more than what first met the eye? And he'd been in the army, where fitness had probably been drilled into him.

"Happy birthday," he said and kissed her neck.

It certainly was.

ADAM SAT ON THE SIDE of Sara's bed, watching her sleep. Even with her hair tousled, she was the most beautiful woman he'd ever seen. How had he not realized that the first time he'd seen her? And it wasn't just her physical beauty that attracted him. It was her dedication to being a good mother to two little girls who might have otherwise been lost. The way she'd made love to him like she didn't have any doubts about him, like he was the best thing to ever walk into her life. Even that part of her that urged her to be selfless, to put her life on the line for others if need be.

He admired it all. Maybe he even loved it all.

And it all scared him half to death.

He needed to get away for a little while, make sure he wasn't making a mistake—for both of their sakes. She didn't know he was damaged goods. He couldn't help thinking that she deserved better. Sure, he was feeling less like a lone wolf these days, but could he really be the type of responsible, giving man she needed?

She might need time to reassess, too. Desire had gotten the better of them, but they both had to be sure before they took things any further. He didn't want to hurt her or the girls again.

She stirred beneath the blankets, enough to make him want to forget his entire line of thought and crawl back into bed with her. He had the sneaky suspicion that he could make love to her a million times and it wouldn't be nearly enough.

He watched as she opened her eyes. She looked sleepy as she smiled at him.

"Is it morning?"

"Technically. I better go before your girls wake up and you have uncomfortable explaining to do when they see my car still in the driveway."

She lifted her head and looked at the clock, then back at him. "You don't have to go yet."

Dang the woman. She had to know how hard it would be for him to resist the invitation in her words. Rarely had he done anything more difficult. He lifted his hand to her cheek and caressed it with his thumb.

"If I get back in that bed, neither of us is going to make it to work on time."

She smiled. "We could call in sick."

He laughed. "Sara Greene, I think you have a little bit of wicked in you." He smiled. "Not that I mind."

Sara lifted herself to a sitting position, holding the sheet up to her chest. What a pity.

"Thanks for last night," she said.

"I could say the same thing," he said. "It felt like my birthday, too."

She laughed just before he captured her mouth with his. The sheet slid from between them, tempting Adam to within an inch of his life. With a growl, he pulled himself away and stood. He didn't know what to say, hadn't faced this situation in a long time. Normally, it was a kiss and a quick goodbye after sex. This wasn't the same—another sign he had to get out of here and think, let her do the same. But how? Did he just turn around and leave?

"You better go get some sleep. Hate to hear of you sleeping on that oh-so-taxing job of yours," she teased, saving him from an uncomfortable exit at the same time.

"I give the woman great sex, and she insults my career," he said, shaking his head.

She lifted her hand, making a so-so gesture. "Mediocre sex."

Though he needed to stay away from her, he took several steps forward and sank on one knee onto the bed, then pulled her naked body into his arms, kissed her thoroughly. She moaned, setting him on fire for her again. He lifted his lips.

"A woman doesn't moan like that after 'mediocre' sex."

He expected a teasing argument, perhaps a jab in the ribs. Instead, she lifted her body against his.

"You're right," she whispered, then kissed him to the point of turning his willpower to pudding.

To hell with good intentions. He wanted her again, and she seemed to be of the same mind. Who was he to deny her?

SARA COULDN'T WIPE the smile off her face. Not when she woke to find the bed still warm where Adam had lain after they'd made love again. Not as she'd taken a shower and dressed. Not even when Ruby came through the side door with the girls, the former with a knowing grin on her face.

"Hi, Mommy!" Lilly said as she launched herself at Sara. "I missed you."

Sara tried to ignore the twinge of guilt, telling herself she deserved time for herself on occasion.

"Have a nice date?" Tana asked, a little too much awareness in her young eyes.

"Yes, thanks. It was late when I came home though, so Ruby suggested you sleep at her house."

Sara didn't like the idea that Tana might suspect what had happened the night before. Sure, she was only thirteen, but she wasn't as blissfully unaware of some things as Sara might like.

"Go on, get ready for school," Sara said as she nodded down the hall.

When both girls had disappeared to their respective rooms, Sara busied herself popping bagels into the toaster and retrieving cream cheese from the fridge. She refused to look at Ruby.

"Well, how was it?" Ruby asked.

"We had a nice time. Went to movie in the park, had a picnic. Even had a birthday candle on a brownie."

"Sounds romantic. And then?"

"And then he brought me home." Sara made the mistake of making eye contact with her neighbor.

"Come on, have a heart. Give an old lady a vicarious thrill."

Sara crossed her arms and faced Ruby. "You are incorrigible."

"Why? Inside this grandma's body beats the heart of a much younger woman."

Sara laughed, then glanced toward the hallway before meeting Ruby's eyes again. "It was wonderful."

Ruby clapped her hands once. "Well, I suspected it would be. I mean, that boy has the body for it."

Sara rolled her eyes and turned to retrieve the bagels from the toaster. No matter how much she scolded Ruby, she couldn't deny her friend was right. Adam Canfield had a body she doubted she'd ever tire of seeing, touching, holding. Add to that his layer of kindness, and…well, how was she going to get him out of her mind and the goofy grin off her face long enough to go to work?

She barely corraled the smile, but memories of the night before and all her interactions with Adam accompanied her throughout the day. It was difficult to concentrate on tracking down burglars or investigating a report of illegal gambling at a resort when memories of how Adam had felt as they'd made love kept popping into her mind.

She started watching the clock for quitting time a full two hours before the official end of her day. Had she ever done that?

Sara released the pen she'd been using to fill out a report and faced the fact that she was falling for Adam, and falling hard. An odd cocktail of scariness and excitement swished around inside her. Could he be the one she'd been looking for all this time?

She tried to picture Adam at home in her house, being a dad to her daughters, being responsible. She bit her bottom lip when she realized the image still didn't quite seem to fit.

But oh how she wanted it to. How could she not experience another night like last night again? If she found that responsible, paternal type, would he make her feel as utterly complete as Adam had?

By the time the clock finally inched its way to 5:00 p.m., Sara was literally aching to see Adam again. Putting her responsible, mommy self aside for a little while, she headed to the Beach Bum, where she suspected she would find him. But when she arrived, his usual stool was occupied by a man she didn't know—a tourist, if his sunburn was any indication.

"Looking for Adam?" Suz asked when she saw her.

"Yeah. He around?"

"Nah. He skipped out a while ago. Said he had something to do tonight. Figured he had another date with you."

Okay, she would not read too much into Suz's words, either positive or negative. He'd mentioned their date, but he had other plans tonight. Well, what did she expect? Him to put his life on hold so he could spend all his free time with her? No. That was silly and juvenile.

This was actually good. After not being with the girls at all last night, they needed a girls-only night. Maybe she'd take them to see a movie, indulge in a humongous bucket of popcorn.

She really tried not to think about Adam as she drove through Horizon Beach toward home, but it didn't work. She scanned parking lots, the windows of businesses, the surrounding streets for any sign of him. She felt about fourteen with her first big crush.

She might have missed the wreck on Palm Street if she hadn't been searching so diligently. The pickup truck hit the Corvette as it stopped at the stop sign at Palm and Canal. Patrol would be en route soon, but still she pulled over to see if anyone was hurt.

By the time she parked, called in the accident and got out, the drivers of the two other vehicles had exited and were yelling at each other.

"Don't you stupid rednecks know what a stop sign is?" the driver of the Corvette screamed at the driver of the truck, Bonnie Shouse, well known to Horizon Beach's patrol officers because of her inability to hold her liquor.

Bonnie yelled back a few choice words, enough for Sara to determine that she was thankfully sober today. In fact, from the look and sound of things, it was the driver of the yellow Corvette, in his golf shirt and khaki shorts, who seemed to have tossed back a few.

Just great.

"Everyone, calm down. An officer will be here shortly, and we'll get everything sorted out."

"I don't need any cop to sort this out," the man said. "I can do that myself."

Before Sara could even guess what he was about to do, he whipped a handgun from inside the car and pointed it at Bonnie.

Sara uttered a curse and raised her hands slowly, palms forward, to about waist high. "There's no need for that. It's just an accident, nothing for anyone to get hurt over."

Sara's heart jolted as he pointed the gun in her direction.

"Nothing to get upset over? I just bought this car

two days ago. And now this piece of white trash not only ruins it, but my vacation as well."

Granted, Bonnie wasn't on Sara's Christmas card list, but she didn't deserve this jerk's treatment of her.

"Sir, you need to put down the gun," Sara said with her firm cop tone.

"Or what? Maybe I get rid of the trash and the nosy bitch at the same time." The man lifted the gun and pointed it right at Sara's thundering heart.

Chapter Twelve

Adam caught himself whistling as he stepped out of Hearts and Flowers Florist. He'd allowed himself nearly a full day to let regret or the urge to flee hit him, but neither had. He liked Sara, really liked her. And unless something changed, he wasn't interested in seeing anyone else.

He couldn't remember the last time he'd bought a woman flowers. That, in and of itself, told him how attached he was becoming to her. A hint of worry poked at him, but he shoved it away. Sara wasn't Jessica. Damn it, he wanted to be truly happy again. And right now, Sara made him happy.

He placed the flowers, a mixture of kinds and colors, on the passenger seat of his car and headed for home. He needed a shower before he went over to Sara's, bouquet in hand.

As he approached Palm Street, he noticed cars pulled off to both sides of the road. Must be a wreck. When he drove closer, however, he noticed a man with a raised handgun. Crap, this wasn't good. He faced two people. One appeared to be Bonnie Shouse, she who had perfected the art of barhopping. He couldn't identify the other person until she took a step sideways, placing herself between the man and Bonnie.

He hit the brakes as his heart pounded.

Sara.

The horror of the Humvee accident scorched him. Pain seared his leg like he was reliving his injury all over again.

No! This wasn't Iraq. But, oh God, he was staring at another nightmare in the making. Only this time, he was going to prevent it.

He slammed his gearshift into Park and leapt from the car. Sirens blared somewhere behind him, but he wasn't about to wait for the uniforms to arrive. He was ending this now. He skirted the opposite side of Bonnie's truck, spotted her bags of groceries in the back. Thankfully, she preferred bottled beer to cans. He filched one bottle, gripped the neck and made his way to the front fender of the passenger side. Corvette Guy was too preoccupied waving his gun around and with the alcohol he'd consumed to notice Adam.

Two patrol cars, with sirens screaming, rounded the corner. They distracted the gunman, and Adam lifted the bottle, ready to throw it at the guy's head. He wouldn't miss.

But movement from Sara froze him. He opened his mouth to yell at her to stop, but nothing came out. He'd swear everything shifted into slow motion as she barreled toward the man and dived for his lower half. As they both fell toward the ground, a shot rang out. Adam's whole body jerked as if he'd been the one shot.

Please, no. Not again. His breath felt sharp and painful as he waited to see blood pooling next to Sara.

But no blood appeared. Instead, he heard her curse as she shoved the guy's face into the pavement and yanked his arms behind his back, cuffing him while ignoring his shouts of pain.

The patrolmen rushed past Adam, and still he couldn't move. It wasn't until Sara rose to her feet, dusted herself off and caught his eye, surprise showing in hers, that he came out of his horrible trance. One of the patrolmen asked her a question. When she looked away, Adam turned and somehow retraced his steps to his car.

He sank into his seat just as the last of the energy left his body. He'd watched Sara's life hanging in the balance, and again he'd been unable to protect her. Sure, she'd been able to handle the situation herself, but that didn't make him feel any less helpless. And what about next time? He couldn't lose someone else he loved.

That thought caused his breath to catch. He looked back at her a few more moments as she talked with her fellow officers, letting the truth of it sink in.

Damn if he hadn't fallen head over heels for Detective Sara Greene.

She might hate him for leaving after what she'd just been through, but he couldn't sit here watching her with a man who might have ended her life. He was not going there again, no matter how much he hated the idea of never being with Sara. Why had he thought he'd gotten past the old scars?

Because he'd wanted to believe he had.

He didn't start shaking until he got halfway home. When he pulled in to his driveway, he had to sit in the car for a good five minutes to get himself under control. Even after he went into the house, he couldn't settle down enough to eat or sit still. Nervous energy flowed through him like lightning looking for something to strike. Finally, he changed and headed out for a run, hoping to exhaust himself beyond the ability to think.

The pounding of his feet against pavement did nothing to help the anxiety and anger flooding his veins. Just like he had with the guy who'd hit Sara during the bar fight, he wanted to beat the living daylights out of Corvette Guy for putting her in harm's way. He stopped at the entrance to the beach parking lot and thought back to the day they'd taken the girls there to fly Lilly's new kite. Something had moved inside him that day, some dormant hunger to connect and be needed. Only now did he realize the full extent of it.

Should he walk away for good this time? Could he even do that at this point? The intense desire to check on her, just to see if she was really okay, ate at him. She wouldn't have to know. Her house was only a few blocks away from where he now stood.

Before he could talk himself out of it, he started jogging in that direction. When he made sure she was okay, really okay, maybe he'd have the willpower to walk away for good.

Maybe not.

If fate had been smiling at him, Sara would have been in the yard where he could get a glimpse of her and go. But despite her car being in the driveway, he saw no sign of her. Knowing he might not have the strength to leave if he got too close, he approached the side door anyway.

He knocked. After a few moments, she opened the door. He'd planned to ask if she was okay. Instead, he stepped across the threshold and pulled her into his arms, kissed her with an intensity he hoped didn't scare her but which he needed.

She kissed him back, fiercely, full of her own need.

"Where are the girls?" he managed to ask.

"Ruby took them to a movie."

The final word was barely across her lips when he scooped her up and carried her to her bedroom. They were naked in seconds and joined soon thereafter. They made love with a power and drive he'd never felt, like they both only had minutes to live and this was the last thing they wanted to experience in this life.

When they finished, they lay in a sweaty heap, arms and legs tangled together. He refused to break contact with her. Despite his spent state, he already wanted her again.

"Where did you go earlier?" she asked after they'd both had time to catch their breath.

Adam searched for a lie and grabbed the first one his brain stumbled over. "I figured you'd be tied up for a long time, reports and all that."

"Oh."

He hated the sound of doubt in her voice, but what was he supposed to do? He shouldn't even be here, in her bed again. What happened to his walking away?

He endured the silence until he couldn't stand it anymore. He swallowed and divulged at least some of what was bottled up inside him. "When I saw him pointing that gun at you, it scared me to death."

"Have to admit, it scared me, too."

Adam lifted to his elbow and looked down at her, the incredible, beautiful woman he was pretty sure he loved. "Then why do you do it?"

"Someone has to."

"But why you?"

She stared up at him, searching his expression as if looking for deeper meaning. "Because I like helping people. Because I'm good at figuring out who did what." She smiled. "I play a mean game of Clue."

He lay back down and stared at the ceiling, wondering... If she had any other job in the world, would he still be debating with himself over maybe staying with her long-term?

"I should go before your girls get home."

This time, she raised up on an elbow and looked down at him, pushed strands of hair behind her ear. "I don't want you to go."

She ran her hand across his chest, causing him to grit his teeth. She had to know what it did to him, how powerless he was to resist her.

They made love again—the sweet and tender kind. The kind where you drifted off to sleep afterward in a blissful haze.

At least until a nightmare woke you.

Adam jerked awake, sweating, his heart pounding. The damn dream had found him again. Only this time, it wasn't Jessica whose lifeless face stared back at him in that Humvee. It was Sara's.

SARA WOKE SUDDENLY, prepared to defend the girls against whatever danger had roused her. It took a few postsleep seconds to remember the girls weren't home and that Adam was with her. At least he had been.

She glanced toward the open bedroom door just as he disappeared down the hallway. She grabbed a robe and threw it around herself as she followed him. It wasn't the side door she heard clicking shut, but rather the one that led to the backyard. She found him standing at the edge of the deck, his face pointed into a strong westerly wind that promised a storm later.

"What's wrong?" Even in the half-light, she could tell he was sweating.

He was quiet for so long, she didn't think he was going to answer. Finally, he heaved a deep breath.

"Just a bad dream."

It had to be a pretty bad dream to propel him out of bed and out of the house. She thought of how she'd told him earlier that she liked to help people. At this moment she wanted to help no one more than him. Because instinct told her there was something deeper to this dream than a one-time product of the subconscious.

She slid her hand into his. "Tell me about it." She said it so softly the wind nearly stole her words. Only the slight squeeze he gave her hand told her that he'd heard.

Again, it took him several long moments to decide to reply. "I told you I was in the army. Did two tours in Iraq, among other hot, dusty places." He stopped, then inhaled deeply before letting the air out again. "I met a girl, an aid worker. Jessica. She was beautiful, funny, didn't once complain about how hot it was or how crappy the food was sometimes." He paused again and looked up at the sky despite the fact clouds had obscured the stars.

"And you fell for her," she said, trying her best not to let him talking about another woman bother her.

He nodded.

But he wasn't with her now, so something had happened. Nothing good.

"We were in a caravan, taking Jessica and some other aid workers to a village outside Kirkuk. One minute we're all laughing at each other's dirty jokes, the next we hit a roadside bomb."

Sara squeezed his hand more tightly, knowing where this story was going now. She nearly told him he didn't have to continue, but she suspected he needed to say it all out loud, that maybe he hadn't told anyone.

"I only remember seeing one thing before I passed out. Jessica's lifeless eyes staring back at me."

"Oh, Adam, I'm so sorry."

"I woke up five days later, and they told me I was the only one to survive in our Humvee. And I don't know why."

Sara slid around in front of him and raised her hand to his cheek. "There doesn't always have to be a why. Bad things just happen sometimes. There's no rhyme or reason."

"But it shouldn't have happened to her. I was the one in the uniform, the one carrying a gun. I was the one who should have been cut in half, not her."

"It's not your fault."

He met her eyes. "I know that in my mind, but my

heart never got the message." He lifted his hand and caressed her cheek. "That's why I live my life the way I do—carefree, no responsibility, no attachments." He looked at her in a way that made her feel loved and sad all at the same time. "That's why it's hard for me to be with a woman who puts herself in harm's way."

Sara stepped closer and placed her hand on his chest. "But you're still here."

He sighed. "I keep telling myself to stay away, and I can't."

After what he'd just told her, Sara didn't want for his words to make her happy. But they did. Maybe he felt as intensely for her as she did about him. Maybe despite both of their reservations, they could make this work. The fact that she loved him blossomed in her mind like a field of beautiful flowers.

"I feel the same way."

He wrapped her in his arms and pulled her against the length of his body. "I don't know if I can worry about the safety of someone I care about again."

Sara leaned back to look up into his eyes. "This isn't a war zone in the Middle East."

"But you're a cop, and cops get killed all the time." He framed one side of her face with a strong hand, a hand that had explored her body only a short time ago. "I've seen you dive off a pier and get punched in a bar fight. And today you were nearly shot."

"But I wasn't. Lots of police officers go their entire careers without serious injury. And sometimes people go to a restaurant and get gunned down. It doesn't mean we all stop going out to eat."

He let go and took a few steps, then leaned his palms against the deck railing. "It's not the same."

"You're right, it's not." She thought about her next words, considered whether she should say them, finally decided she had to be honest if there was any hope for them. "But it's better than living my life superficially."

He looked back at her. "You think that's what I'm doing?"

"Isn't it?"

Adam returned his gaze to her dark yard and shrugged. "Maybe."

"Just because you lose someone doesn't mean you cut yourself off from the world and stop caring." She searched for the words to get through to him, to break the shell he'd erected around himself. Or had she already cracked it? Is that why he'd even told her about Jessica? He cared, whether he wanted to or not. She just didn't know how much.

Sara moved to the railing and leaned back against it next to Adam. "I could have chosen the same path as you, but I decided to take the other fork in the road."

"You lost someone?"

"My mom."

"What happened?"

"She left when I was young. Just packed her bags and left me and my dad behind. Dad raised me on his own. He was a life-long cop, Memphis patrol. A real guy's guy, you know. But he did the best he could to raise a girl."

"Sounds like a great guy."

"He was. But he never got over Mom leaving him, always thought she'd stroll back into our lives someday. Believed it until the day he died. I never quite forgave her for that."

"I'm sorry."

She shook her head. "It's part of the past now."

"Is your mom still alive?"

"I don't know."

"You've never looked for her?"

"No. I had to cut that tie, even let the resentment go so I could move forward. It was holding me back from really living the life I wanted."

Adam shifted and crossed his arms. "Did your dad want you to become a cop like him?"

"He never said. I didn't really make the decision until after he was gone." Sara looked out into the darkness beyond the light shed by the house next door. "I went to college, changed majors a couple of times. Even did some student teaching. But nothing felt right, not until I decided to go to the academy. Being with other officers, it felt a bit like a family, especially since I didn't have one anymore."

"That's how the army felt for a while. But after

the accident...well, I took the medical discharge and ran as fast and as far as I could."

"But you didn't find any peace."

He shook his head slowly. "No."

"I'm sorry you've lived with this."

"Hey, I think we just proved that I'm not the only one with dark spots in my life."

"True. Don't get me wrong. I could have given in to the hate I sometimes felt toward my mother, toward fate for my dad having a heart attack at his desk one month shy of retirement. But something inside of me just made all those negative feelings dissolve one day. I still can't explain it. I just knew I wanted to live as positive a life as I could. I wanted to be happy, have a family that was close and loving. And I acknowledged that I did want to make police work my career. Not be a street cop like my dad was, but in the field nonetheless."

"How did you decide on detective?"

She stared at the pot of geraniums next to the back door. "It kind of chose me. I solved my first case before I ever stepped foot in the academy. Our neighbor was a victim of a hit-and-run. I started asking questions and figured out who did it, found the guy and called the police."

Adam turned to face her. "How old were you?"

"Twenty."

"So I guess there's no chance of you giving it all up to work in the kite shop, huh?"

She gave him a half smile. "No." A few moments passed in silence. "I understand why you don't like to be responsible for anyone, but sometimes it's really rewarding. Bringing Lilly and Tana into my life, trying to be the mother they deserve—it's the best thing I've ever done. I couldn't love them more if they were my own flesh and blood."

"From what I've seen, they love you, too."

She smiled. "We have a good life." She was determined to be happy with their trio if that was the way it was meant to be, but she couldn't help hoping that there was a special spot for Adam in that family dynamic. If not, she'd enjoy what time they had and hope tonight wasn't the end of it. She turned toward him. "I'm glad I let you in."

Adam offered a small smile with a bittersweet tinge. "I am, too." He kissed her, a soft meeting of lips that lasted far too short a time. "I better go."

She didn't want him to leave, but he was right. Ruby and the girls would be home any minute. Unable to let him go just yet, she clasped his hand. "Remember what I said. You have a lot of life left. You deserve to enjoy it."

"Yes, ma'am," he said softly before he gave her one last peck on the lips then stepped off the deck and disappeared into the night.

She fought the new panic that she'd scared him away with her talk of family and her dedication to her job. If she had, she'd have to live with it.

Just as soon as she figured out how to live without the part of her heart this unexpected man had claimed as his own.

Chapter Thirteen

Sara hurried out the door, late for work. As she reached her car, her cell rang. She recognized Lara Stephens's number at the Social Services office. She answered the call as she opened the car door.

"Hey, Lara, what's up?"

Hesitation on Lara's end sounded a warning that what she had to say wasn't going to be good. "I wanted to let you know that David Taylor has been returned to his father."

"What?" Sara couldn't believe what she was hearing. "Why? When?"

"This morning. The ruling came down that there wasn't enough evidence to hold him in state custody."

"Lara, that boy is in danger."

"You don't think I know that? I argued against this, but I was overruled."

Sara stood motionless, too stunned to know what to say or do next.

"I'm sorry, Sara. I thought you should know." Lara hung up and left the sorrow of her words ringing in Sara's ear.

Sorry wasn't going to do the boy any good if his father wanted to punish him for running away and bringing the police into the situation. Sara's stomach rolled, threatening to make her eggs and toast stage an unwelcome reappearance.

On top of that, Adam's car screeched to a stop at the curb. She knew as soon as he unfolded himself from the driver's seat that he wasn't there for any romantic reasons.

"What the hell were you all thinking?"

She shook her head. "I just heard myself. Lara can't believe it, either. She fought against it."

"She didn't do a very good job."

"Adam, that's not fair. The ruling came from higher-ups."

"I don't care where it came from, it's wrong." Adam's face was flushed and strained. He looked on the verge of exploding.

"I know. But…I can't do anything." She'd never felt so helpless in her life.

"Well, I can," he said, then started to turn away.

She grabbed his arm. "Adam, don't do something stupid."

"I think others have a corner on the stupid market."

"Please. It won't do David any good if you get yourself arrested."

He pulled out of her grip and paced several steps. "How does this happen? I turned him over to you because the system was supposed to keep him safe."

"I know," she said, on the verge of tears at the thought of David back home, at how he must be feeling betrayed. How could she answer Adam when she didn't understand why the government machine acted like it did sometimes?

They stood in awkward silence for several interminable seconds before she couldn't stand it anymore.

"How did you find out?" she asked.

"I called David, thought maybe I'd take the kid fishing today since I have the day off."

Something shifted in her heart. This man who had held himself away from others had made a connection with this boy, only to see him ripped away, too. Nobody won in this situation.

"I'm sorry," she said again. She couldn't think of anything else to say.

Adam looked back at her, less anger reflected on his face this time. "I know."

She wanted to walk to him, wrap her arms around him and have him do the same to her. But instead they stood staring at each other until Adam moved to leave.

"I'll talk to you later. I'm not going to be the best of company for a while."

"Okay."

Give him time. It had worked before. Hopefully, it would again.

THE URGE TO DRIVE NORTH and check on David, to pummel his father for hurting the boy, didn't leave Adam no matter how much he tried to focus on other things. He called David several times, but no one ever picked up the phone. When he talked to Sara, she reported the same result when she'd made attempts.

He didn't truly blame Sara for the situation. He knew what the chain of command was like and how little pull those on the lower rungs really had. No, it was himself he blamed. Yet again, he'd let someone down. It seemed like it'd become his purpose in life.

When Adam arrived home three nights after David's return to his father, the sound of gagging greeted him as he stepped inside the door. What the...? He edged toward the bathroom, which seemed to be the source of the sound. There he found someone with his head hanging over the toilet in the dark.

Adam turned on the light, then cursed under his breath. David jerked back, his eyes frantic. His face glistened with sweat, and he looked too pale.

"It's okay. It's just me." Adam wetted a wash-cloth and handed it to David. It seemed all the boy could do to lift his hand to take it. "He hit you again?" No sense in skirting the issue.

"Yeah." He sounded weak.

"I'll kill him."

David's eyes grew impossibly wide, like one of those anime characters the kids liked now. "No!"

The boy became so agitated that Adam retreated

a step. "Okay. I'm not going anywhere. But you need a doctor. You might be injured internally if you're throwing up."

"No. I just came down with something." David leaned back against the wall and closed his eyes. "I'll be okay. I'll leave as soon as I feel a little better."

Adam leaned against the sink counter. "The hell you will."

"I don't want to get you into trouble."

"You let me worry about that, okay?" Adam stared at the kid and didn't see any obvious marks, just dark circles under his eyes, a pale complexion and the appearance of having aged ten years since he saw him last. He wondered if the kid was really sick or just reacting badly to everything that had happened to him.

When several moments passed without further retching, David attempted to stand, his arms shaking as he pressed against the toilet. Adam stepped forward to help.

"Okay, off to bed you go." Instead of steering him toward the couch, he aimed David toward his bedroom.

"I'm not taking your room." David tried to dig in his heels, but he was weaker than weak.

"You're not in much shape to argue, are you?"

Adam managed to get David into the bed and covered him up not only with the sheet, but also two blankets since the chills had set in during their journey from the bathroom. He brought in a fresh glass of water and set it on the nightstand. "It might make you puke again, but you have to keep drinking or you'll get more dehydrated."

David nodded almost imperceptibly.

Adam leaned forward and placed his hand on David's forehead. Clammy and quite warm.

"Adam?"

"Yeah?"

"I'm sorry for breaking in. I...I didn't know where else to go."

"You're safe here. And I mean it this time."

David swallowed hard. "I hit him."

"Your dad?"

"Yeah. Not enough to worry about, but enough to get away from him."

"Good." Adam didn't care about all the not fighting violence with violence arguments now. He was just glad the bastard had received a bit of his own medicine.

Once he got David settled, he wandered into the kitchen and started to pull a beer from the fridge. He stopped, grabbed a Coke instead. He had a feeling he wasn't going to get any sleep tonight. Not only did he need to check on David throughout the night, but there was also too much rolling around in his head like a load of clothes in a dryer. Not the least of which was the strange, satisfied feeling he'd had when he'd left the bedroom.

Face it, Canfield. You like helping the kid. It makes you feel human again.

He cursed and wandered out to sit on the porch, to lose himself in the night. If he listened hard, he could hear the sound of waves in the distance. They didn't soothe him tonight.

He wasn't calling the cops this time, and that meant hiding David from Sara. But David wasn't going back to within yelling distance of his father, even if Adam had hide the kid until he was eighteen.

Even if it cost him Sara.

TANA STROLLED INTO the police station and dropped into the chair next to Sara's desk.

"Tough day?" Sara asked, trying not to smile.

"Long and boring. And art got canceled because of a pep rally."

Tana wasn't the pep rally type.

"Oh, the nerve."

Tana stuck her tongue out at Sara.

"Classy."

Tana rolled her eyes and bent over to pull several boxes of chocolates from her backpack. She passed them out to the people at the station who had ordered them from her while Sara finished working on the file she had open.

"I've got Adam's candy, too," Tana said when she returned to Sara's desk just as she was shutting down her computer. "Can we run it by his place?"

"Sure." Even though Adam hadn't been by in the past few days, they'd talked on the phone. He didn't sound angry with her anymore. At least he hadn't totally disappeared this time, even if he did sound distant, as though David's return to his father was still bothering him. She could understand that.

But surely he wouldn't mind if they stopped by to drop off his candy. She had to admit, she wanted to see him in person, to try to judge what he was feeling by facial expressions, not just intonations on the phone.

When her phone rang, she picked it up. "Detective Greene."

"Sara, it's Lara. I'm glad I caught you. David Taylor is missing again."

"Oh, God," she said. She hated that her first thought was that Mr. Taylor had done something worse to his son this time. "How long?"

"Evidently two days ago, but his father didn't report it. We didn't know until we came up here to do a follow-up visit. His dad said they had an argument, and David ran. But not before he whacked his dad with a shovel."

"Why didn't his dad report him missing?"

"He said he decided the kid wasn't worth the trouble. That he'd come home when he got hungry. This guy is a real piece of work."

Sara gritted her teeth but did her best to stay calm because of Tana's presence.

After the phone conversation, Sara rebooted her computer.

"What's wrong?" Tana asked.

She glanced at her daughter. "David Taylor's run away from home again." She transferred all of David's information into a new case file, then sent messages to everyone else in the department about David's renewed status as missing. After turning off the computer for a second time, she and Tana headed to the car.

She dreaded telling Adam about David. He'd feared something like this would happen. She didn't relish the idea of trying to keep Adam from ripping the elder Taylor apart.

When they arrived at Adam's house, he met them at the door but didn't invite them in. Sara tried not to be hurt, but her efforts failed her.

"Your candy came in," Tana said as she extended the box toward him.

"Thanks," he said as he took it.

They all stood there for a few awkward seconds before Sara said, "David has run away again."

He didn't even look surprised. "I'll keep an eye out for him." Why did his voice sound so flat, so emotionless? She didn't want to see him revert back to the detached state he'd been living in when they met.

"Please do. He could be hurt. His dad isn't saying."

"That's because he's a coward."

The sound of David's voice surprised Sara. She glanced past Adam to see David standing inside.

"I'm not going back," he said.

"I'll make sure of that," she said.

"You shouldn't make a promise you can't keep," Adam said.

She looked at him, tried to find some shred of the man she'd made love to, who'd opened up to her about his devastating past. He seemed so very far away.

"Can we come in?" she finally asked when he still didn't offer. "You know I can't just walk away."

"I don't want Adam to get in trouble. I knew I shouldn't have stayed so long." David sounded so forlorn as he turned and disappeared into the house that Sara's heart broke for him.

Tana must have heard it, too, because she shoved her way past Adam and followed David. Adam stepped back to allow Sara inside. She walked into the house in time to see Tana perch on the edge of the coffee table near where David sat.

"You can trust Mom," Tana said. "What happened before wasn't her fault. She hated it."

The bunched muscles of David's body eased at Tana's words. Having someone his own age, a peer, to talk to might make this easier. Someone he'd trust more than the adults who had failed him.

"I'll do everything I can for you, David," Sara said. "But I have to take you into custody."

"No." Adam's answer was cold, hard, unyielding.

"No matter what's happened, he's still under age. It's still illegal to harbor a runaway."

Adam looked at David. "Those bruises still on your side?"

David glanced toward Tana, clearly embarrassed.

"Hey, if it makes you feel any better, my parents are drug dealers who skipped the country without me so they wouldn't be arrested," Tana said.

Sara wanted to hug Tana close for helping to ease the way with David, for using her own awful experience to make it easier for him to open up. It worked because he stood and raised the left side of his T-shirt. Sara didn't even have to move closer to him to see the angry purple marks the size of a man's fist.

Her anger flared. "No authority can possibly put you back with someone who has done that to you. I know you have no reason to trust me after what happened, but I promise you I will stand right next to you if I have to until a ruling is made that you don't ever have to go back."

"What about Adam?" The concern in the boy's voice touched her, and in that moment she determined to try to help Adam, too. After all, he'd only been trying to protect the boy from further harm, taking on a type of responsibility he used to maintain he didn't want. Another layer of Adam Canfield peeled back, another thing for her to love about him.

"I'll see what I can do. I need you to get your things together if you have anything else here."

David looked at Adam, who stood for several long moments before nodding his agreement.

Tana squeezed his hand. "Come on, I'll help."

When the two of them rose and started gathering David's things, Sara walked into Adam's kitchen, forcing him to follow her.

"What were you planning?" she asked quietly so the kids wouldn't hear her.

"That I would keep him here until he turned eighteen if that was the only way to make sure that bastard didn't hurt him again."

Sara looked up into Adam's eyes. Law or no law, how could she argue with that? Wouldn't she do the same for Tana or Lilly if necessary? She sighed. "I don't want you to say anything more than absolutely necessary, understand?"

"I'll say whatever will help the kid."

"Then say nothing you don't have to. Trust me." *Trust me now, even if you didn't before.* "This is serious."

"I know." He looked over his shoulder toward the living room, where Tana kept up a steady stream of largely one-sided conversation. "I just want him to be safe."

In that moment, Sara could see him as a father, even one good enough for her precious daughters. But would he ever see himself in that role?

"I'll do everything I can for him," she said.

He returned his gaze to hers, and she saw a determination there she'd never seen before.

"So will I."

ADAM WATCHED AS Sara walked back into the living room, as she and Tana did their best to reassure David. As he watched the boy head for the door, his protective instincts, long buried, nearly over-whelmed him. He'd thought them incinerated under the merciless Middle Eastern skies, but it seemed they had a bit of life in them yet.

For years, he'd lived with the knowledge that he had been a miserable failure in his protector role. But so had David's father, so had his own dad. Tana's and Lilly's parents. He didn't want to be like any of those people. Maybe he didn't have to be, if he was willing to try again. Get back up on the horse, so to speak.

When David's eyes met his, so full of fear and doubt, the last vestiges of Adam's reluctance to be responsible for anyone else burned away. This kid needed a protector, and damned if Adam didn't want to assume that duty.

He rounded the end of the bar separating the kitchen from the living room and gripped David's shoulder. "Don't worry. I'll be there for you, every step of the way."

Adam caught the look in Sara's eyes, one of ad-miration and bone-deep belief in his words. She couldn't have given him a better gift.

But then she turned away without a goodbye, without any word at all.

"THINKING ABOUT ADAM?"

Sara looked up from the pot of spaghetti she was stirring, at Tana leaning against the door frame that led from the kitchen to the living room.

"David, actually." But weren't the two of them now tied together in her mind?

"How is he?"

"As well as can be expected."

"They're not going to send him back to his dad again, are they?"

Sara shook her head. "There was enough evidence to keep him in state custody this time." The guilt over what he'd endured after his return to his father ate at her even though it hadn't been her call.

Tana eased into the room and came to stand next to Sara. "Have you talked to Adam since the other night?"

"I've been busy." Sara added a little salt to the boiling pot.

"The past four days have been so busy that you couldn't call him?"

"He hasn't called me, either." Okay, that sounded more bitter than she'd intended.

Tana just stood there, staring at her as if she'd encountered the world's dumbest animal, until Sara couldn't stand it anymore.

"What?"

"You're a detective. You figure it out."

Sara watched Tana spin on her heel and leave

the room, until the pot boiling over drew her attention back to the stove. She muttered an oath and grabbed the pot holders to move the pot to a cool burner.

Someone knocked on the door, and she noticed Tana answering it. When she tossed the pot holders back onto the counter, she turned to see Tana step back from the door and make for the hallway.

"The guy who didn't call you is here," she said, a wicked gleam in her eyes.

Sara gave her a hard stare, promising some sort of retribution later. But first, she had to deal with Adam—and the way her heart was thundering at seeing him again. She admitted to herself that she'd missed him, that it hurt that he hadn't called.

But Tana was right. She hadn't left Adam's place with a "call me" vibe. Maybe he wasn't cutting and running. Maybe he'd just been giving her time. Well, he was evidently done waiting.

She couldn't seem to move as she watched him close the door and walk toward her. Even with dark circles under his eyes and an unsure expression on his face, he looked wonderful. After everything that had happened the past few days, was she crazy to think about grabbing him by the front of his shirt and dragging his lips down to hers?

"I would have called, but I seem to be the 'drop in unannounced' sort of guy." His teasing sounded halfhearted, like it was no longer effortless.

Her face warmed when she thought about the last time he'd done exactly that and where they'd ended up.

"You certainly don't play by the rules most of the time."

He shoved his hands in his pants pockets, and for the first time she noticed he had on khaki slacks and a green button-up shirt.

"Things change," he said.

She tilted her head slightly. "How so?"

"I've spent the day talking to all kinds of people with official titles."

Sara's breath caught. "What? I didn't..."

"I know you didn't say anything about how long David had been at my house. Otherwise, I doubt I'd still be walking around a free man."

Sara shook her head. "Then who were you talking to?"

"The child advocate, a nice lady at the foster care system who sets up training and background checks, and a lot of other people who push paper for a living."

Sara stared at Adam for a moment and realized the take-no-responsibility guy she'd talked to at the Beach Bum that day wasn't the one standing in her kitchen.

"You're going to foster him?"

"Going to try. Looks like these things take awhile. But, hey, I've been in the military. I'm well acquainted with government red tape."

"Are you sure about this? Because David's been through enough. He doesn't deserve to get his hopes up only to have them dashed if you change your mind, decide the responsibility thing really isn't for you." She saw the disappointment in his expression, but she had to know. Not only because David would get his hopes up, but because hers were on the verge of skyrocketing, too.

"Not everyone walks away, Sara."

She should let it go, accept this new Adam at face value, but something in her couldn't. Some insecure part of her kept picking at the scab, wanting incontrovertible proof than he'd changed, that he was truly the man she so desperately wanted him to be.

"But you already did once. You walked away from life, responsibility, from caring too deeply because you were afraid to."

He held her gaze for a few moments before saying, "You're right. But I wouldn't start this if I didn't mean to finish it." He paused. "I hope you come to believe that."

She didn't know what to say, what to believe. Had he been talking about his relationship with her as much as his plans to foster David? Even as she watched him turn and head for the door, she couldn't form words for what she was feeling inside—that she didn't want to live life without him in it.

When the door clicked closed softly, she jumped as if it had slammed shut on a beautiful future.

Prompted to movement, she ran to the door and jerked it open. But it was too late. She watched as Adam drove away.

Chapter Fourteen

The house's red front door opened to reveal Elizabeth Alston, whom Sara had gotten to know through the foster care program. She and her husband were fostering David while his case worked its way through the system.

"Sara, it's so good to see you," Elizabeth said as she smiled and pulled Sara into a quick hug. "And Tana, girl, you are taller every time I see you." Elizabeth ruffled Lilly's hair before motioning them all inside. "Ben is showing David the fine art of grilling steaks out back."

David spotted them as they neared the sliding-glass door that led to the back patio. He smiled and offered an awkward wave.

Sara touched Tana's arm. "Go on and introduce Lilly. I'll be out in a minute."

Tana took Lilly's hand and headed outside. Sara watched as the three of them retreated to lawn chairs at the edge of the patio.

"How's he doing?" Sara asked Elizabeth as the other woman retrieved cold sodas from the refrigerator.

"Really well. Honestly, I think we would try to become his permanent fosters if Adam hadn't already expressed interest."

"You think he's serious?" She really needed a third-party opinion that wasn't one of her daughters' or matchmaking Ruby's.

"Judging by the fact he comes to see David every day, I'd say so. I'd also say it's odd that the two of them bonded so quickly, but I can see how that would happen with David. He's a great kid."

"Yeah." Plus, Adam and David had bonded over more than the single day she'd led everyone to believe David had been at Adam's house. She was glad she wasn't so by the book that the slight misdirection of the truth bothered her. Sometimes, adhering to the rules wasn't the best course of action.

"Actually, Adam should be here any minute."

Sara jerked her attention from where Lilly was playing patty-cake with David, who was laughing at her.

Elizabeth smiled wide. "I heard the two of you were an item."

Sara lowered her eyes. "We... went out a few times."

"Sara, honey, I love you, but you're a terrible liar."

"I'm not lying."

Elizabeth put her arm around Sara and ushered

her toward the patio. "Not technically. But there's more to the story than a few casual dates."

"How do you know that?"

Elizabeth stopped and took a step away to look at Sara with an amused expression. "You do remember what I do for a living, right?"

Sara sighed as she admitted she'd been accurately pegged by an ace psychologist. Elizabeth had an uncanny knack for reading people—thus the reason the police department contracted her services every now and again.

"If it helps, I'm pretty sure he's hung up on you, too."

Sara raised her gaze to Elizabeth's. "What makes you say that?"

"I heard David ask him about you one day, if he'd talked to you, and I swear the man blushed."

Sara laughed a little. "Okay, I think you're losing your touch. Adam Canfield doesn't blush."

"Stranger things have been known to happen," Elizabeth said as she opened the sliding-glass door and stepped outside.

Sara only half heard the conversations going on around her for the next several minutes as she anticipated seeing Adam again, wondering how he'd react when he saw her. After all, it'd been three days since he'd left her standing in her house, more deeply lonely than she'd ever been. She'd picked up the phone several times but never dialed his number.

And this time, it should be her who made the call. What could she say? What did she want to say?

That she loved him. That she hated every day that went by when she didn't get to hold him, touch him, kiss him.

"Sara."

His voice, so deep and so close, startled her. Only when she forced her gaze up from the grass did she realize she'd been staring at the ground for who knew how long.

"Adam. Hey."

"I didn't know you'd be here."

"Me neither. I mean, I didn't know you'd be here." She felt like all the wrong words were coming out of her mouth. "It's nice to see you."

She thought she saw him relax a little. "You, too."

"Perfect timing, Adam," Ben said as he placed a platter of steaks on the patio table.

Was it? Perfect timing? Sara wanted to drag him away from the others and tell him everything, but she didn't have the opportunity.

Instead, she sat across from him all during the meal and couldn't keep herself from glancing at him every few seconds. He finally caught her, but she didn't look away. And she didn't care that all her feelings were probably naked in her eyes.

Heaven help her if she was wrong, but she thought she saw them reflected back.

A giggle from the opposite end of the table drew

her attention. She noticed the knowing look on Tana's face, then on David's. Even Lilly's wide grin held a touch of awareness. She didn't dare meet Ben's and Elizabeth's eyes.

"This was great," Adam said several minutes later as he wadded his napkin and tossed it onto his plate. "But I've got to get to work. Took the afternoon shift today."

Sara wanted to grab his arm and make him stay until they'd said everything that had been floating unspoken between them. But somehow she restrained herself. And watched him go yet again.

When she redirected her gaze to the other end of the table, Tana and David were leaning close and talking. Why did she get the feeling they were planning something?

"What are you two up to?" she asked.

Tana put on her best innocent face, and David followed her lead quickly but less effectively.

"Nothing," Tana said.

Lilly's giggle gave them away, but even she made as if she were zipping her lips and throwing away the key.

Sara was facing a kid conspiracy.

No MATTER HOW MUCH she grilled the girls over the next twenty-four hours, neither of them broke. Finally, Sara gave up. She'd just deal with whatever mischief they were cooking up when the time came.

Knowing her girls, it wouldn't be too bad. Even though David was a new player in the mix and older, Sara had no doubt that Tana was still the ringleader.

After a long day of work the next day, she arrived at Ruby's to find a note.

> Gone to the beach with the girls. Come over to
> Blue Cove after you change. Ruby.

All she wanted to do was soak in a bubble bath for about an hour, but maybe she and the girls could watch the sunset together. She'd been so wrapped up in Adam lately that she worried she'd been neglecting the girls. Her common sense told her she hadn't, but she guessed that fear of not being the perfect parent wasn't going to go away overnight.

After changing, she headed to the Blue Cove beach access. But when she didn't find Ruby or the girls, her heart sped up. She turned in a quick circle atop the dune, but all she saw was a white table on the beach flanked by a tall tent with white fabric sides blowing in the breeze. She was already dialing her phone as she turned toward the parking lot in time to see Adam pull in beside her car.

The moment he got out of the car, she asked, "Have you seen Ruby or the girls?"

A look of surprise crossed his face. "No. I got a call from David to meet him here."

"David?" Sara looked over her shoulder to the

table, noticed that it appeared to be set for a meal. A flash of Tana and David whispering to each other at Elizabeth and Ben's house helped her realize what was going on just as Adam joined her on top of the dune.

"I think we've been played," she said as she nodded toward the table.

He stared at it for a moment before the truth sank in. Then he smiled. "Well, I'm game if you are."

Sara accepted Adam's offered arm and allowed him to lead her to the table. She had to admit that this setting was really romantic. For that, she was sure she had Ruby to thank. As Adam sat across from her, uncharacteristic nerves fired within her. She tried not to think about where this might end up, especially when she suspected the kids were in that tent several yards away.

But it wasn't the kids or Ruby, not even Elizabeth or Ben, who emerged from the tent. It was a waiter in black slacks, white shirt and black bow tie. He arrived at the side of the table bearing two shrimp cocktails and a bottle of champagne. Sara couldn't find words, but Adam managed to thank the unknown man before he disappeared back into the tent.

For a moment, she thought she could see someone peeking out the side of the tent, but she wasn't sure. She'd go along with all this because she missed Adam, and here he was so close.

He popped the cork on the champagne bottle. She

laughed when the liquid rolled out and down his arm.

Adam shook the excess liquid off his arm. "I never was good at that."

"More of a beer kind of guy, huh?"

He grinned at her. "Yeah."

"How have you been?" she asked, hating that she found talking to him so awkward now.

He shrugged. "Okay. Busy. The state certainly has a lot of hoops to jump through before you can foster a kid."

"It's to protect the kids from bad situations."

"I know," he said as he poured some champagne in her glass.

She lifted the glass and took a drink. "So, you're going to go through with it?"

"Yes. Kid kind of grew on me, I guess." He met her eyes. "Lots of people been doing that lately."

Sara's heart sped up, fueled by hope. "I know what you mean."

She asked him about where he was in the foster process and he responded with details as they ate their shrimp cocktails.

The waiter arrived to remove their dishes just as they finished. "Your main course will be out momentarily."

Sara watched as the waiter retraced his steps.

"Where do you think they got him?" Adam asked.

"I'm sure that's Ruby's doing." She looked back

at Adam, taking a moment to appreciate how wonderful he looked in the slant of setting sun, like some gilded gift to women. To her. "I'm sorry about all this. They're determined to play matchmaker."

"I'm not."

"Not what?" she asked, a lump threatening to form in her throat.

"Sorry." He reached across the table and took her hand in his. "I've missed you."

Sara bit her bottom lip to keep from spilling every single feeling that was swirling inside of her. He didn't even release her when the waiter returned with the main course, a delicious-smelling combination of grilled chicken and steak.

How was she supposed to eat when Adam's thumb was stroking the top of her hand?

Her stomach growled, betraying the hunger she'd temporarily forgotten.

Adam laughed. "Hungry?"

"Apparently, I can never hide that fact," she said as she remembered doing the same thing on movie night in the park. She lowered her gaze to her food.

Despite her hunger, she was only able to take a few bites before her nerves got in the way.

"Your food okay?" Adam asked.

"Yeah. It's just..." She looked up at him. "I'm sorry about the way I acted when you were at my house the other day. I shouldn't have questioned you like I did."

Adam lowered his fork to his plate. "I'm glad you did. It made me examine my reasoning one more time."

"And?"

"And, crazy as it might seem, I don't like the idea of anyone else raising him. I've changed in the past several weeks, in ways I didn't think I ever would. Thanks to you."

"I didn't do anything."

"You liked me, the me behind all the flirting and bluster."

"It's not hard."

Soft music drew their attention, and Sara had to laugh when she saw Tana's iPod dock sitting in the sand outside the tent.

"I think that's our cue to dance." Adam extended his hand.

She went willingly into his arms. Oh, she'd missed this, the wondrous feeling of being encircled in his strong arms, their hearts beating so close together, the male scent of him tickling her nose. She gave in to her yearning and laid her cheek against his chest, closed her eyes and drank in all the sensations of being next to him, listened to the waves and the soft music intertwining.

Sara dropped the barrier she used to protect her heart from further loss and let the truth come out. "I've missed you, too."

Adam stopped dancing and moved so that she faced him. Then he dropped his lips to hers and kissed her like they'd been looking for each other for a thousand years.

When Adam lifted his mouth from hers, he kept her close and ran his hand gently over her windswept hair. "You know, I think our kids might be smarter than we are."

The way he said "our kids" melted her heart, and she knew without a doubt she'd found her Mr. Perfect.

"I love you," she said, no hint of fear or tentativeness in her voice.

He looked startled for a moment, then smiled before capturing her mouth again.

She was still floating on a cloud of satisfaction when she heard Adam chuckle. She looked over her shoulder to see a handmade sign sticking out of the side of the tent that said, "Ask her!"

Ask her what? When she turned back toward Adam, she saw such an intense look of love on his face that it took her breath away.

"I think they've been reading my mind."

Sara's pulse kicked into overdrive as she suddenly knew what was about to happen.

Adam caressed her cheek as softly as the beach breeze. "For a long time, I didn't think I could fall for anyone again. I was wrong."

Sara's heart stopped in anticipation.

"I'm ready to try happily ever after if you are," he said. "I know I'm not perfect, but—"

Sara placed her fingers against his lips, forcing

him to stop speaking. "I've been looking for Mr. Perfect for a long time, and I finally found him. You're perfect to me."

Adam pulled her closer. "I love you, Sara Greene. Will you marry this lowly pier worker?"

Happy tears sprang to Sara's eyes as she said, "Only if you promise to flirt with me forever. I kind of miss it."

"That I can do," he said just before he kissed her to seal the deal.

Voices from inside the tent drew their attention.

"Should we put them out of their misery?" Adam asked.

Sara laughed and nodded.

"You can come out," Adam called out. "She said yes."

The tent threatened to collapse as Tana, David and Lilly ran out, followed by Ruby. As the kids careened into Sara and Adam, squealing with happiness, Sara's heart swelled. She had her family. Life was perfect.

Epilogue

Sara stepped out into a beautiful, bright October day to find her new husband on a ladder reattaching the gutter that had come loose on the corner of her...their house. Feeling mischievous, she whistled in appreciation of the sight before her. Nothing like sexy, sweaty male.

He turned and gave her a crooked grin. "Like the view, huh?"

"Whoever invented the tool belt must have been a woman." She admired how it hung at his waist, accenting his jean-clad assets.

"You just come out to ogle, or can I have one of those glasses of lemonade?"

She held up a glass and wiggled it. "Come and get it."

He growled as he came down the ladder and stalked toward her. "You, Mrs. Canfield, are a tease," he said before lowering his lips to hers for a long kiss that promised more.

When the kiss ended, he took one of the glasses and downed half of the contents, then rolled the cool exterior against his forehead. He looked back at the gutter. "I think I've got it fixed."

"Looks good. You've become quite the handyman around here."

Again with the flirty grin. "I aim to please."

She ignored the innuendo and returned her attention to the back of the house that had now become home to two more people. "What do you think about adding on another room?"

He shrugged. "Maybe. We're doing fine now. I know Tana probably wishes she didn't have to share with Lilly now that David's here, but we'll get by."

"Yeah, but I kind of doubt David is going to want to share with someone who needs to be fed every two hours."

Adam froze then turned slowly toward her, looking like he hadn't heard her correctly.

"A baby?"

She couldn't stop the mile-wide smile that took over her mouth. "Yes. In May."

Adam whooped and pulled her into his arms, lifted her and swung her around. The small ball of worry she'd harbored that this extra responsibility might put him over the edge dissipated. His joy washed over her, making her laugh.

"When does all this newlywed goofiness end?" Tana's question alerted them to the fact that Ruby

and the kids were back from their trip to Destin for
a day of mini golf and riding go-carts.

"Never," Adam teased her.

Sara couldn't stop smiling when Ruby gave her a
look that said she knew something was up.

"Adam and I were just talking about adding another room on to the house," Sara said.

The kids all talked at once.

"Toy room," said Lilly.

"Media room," offered David.

Tana crossed her arms. "Hello, it's so I can have
my own room again."

"Actually," Sara said. "It's going to be a nursery."

Lilly looked confused, but understanding hit
David and Tana at the same time.

"You're having a baby?" Tana said, her face and
voice reflecting wonder.

Sara nodded.

The kids ran forward to envelop her and Adam in
hugs and squeals. She caught Adam's gaze and
hoped her private smile for him reflected how very
much she loved him and their family. And the fact
that he'd become the perfect family man.

* * * * *

Harlequin offers a romance for every mood!
See below for a sneak peek
from our paranormal romance line,
Silhouette® Nocturne™.
Enjoy a preview of REUNION by USA TODAY
bestselling author Lindsay McKenna.

Aella closed her eyes and sensed a distinct shift,
like movement from the world around her to the
unseen world.

She opened her eyes. And had a slight shock at
the man standing ten feet away. He wasn't just any
man. Her heart leaped and pounded. He reminded
her of a fierce warrior from an ancient civilization.
Incan? She wasn't sure but she felt his deep power
and masculinity.

*I'm Aella. Are you the guardian of this sacred
site?* she asked, hoping her telepathy was strong.

Fox's entire body soared with joy. Fox struggled
to put his personal pleasure aside.

*Greetings, Aella. I'm the assistant guardian to
this sacred area. You may call me Fox. How can I be
of service to you, Aella?* he asked.

*I'm searching for a green sphere. A legend says
that the Emperor Pachacuti had seven emerald
spheres created for the Emerald Key necklace. He
had seven of his priestesses and priests travel the
world to hide these spheres from evil forces. It is said*

that when all seven spheres are found, restrung and worn, that Light will return to the Earth. The fourth sphere is here, at your sacred site. Are you aware of it? Aella held her breath. She loved looking at him, especially his sensual mouth. The desire to kiss him came out of nowhere.

Fox was stunned by the request. *I know of the Emerald Key necklace because I served the emperor at the time it was created. However, I did not realize that one of the spheres is here.*

Aella felt sad. Why? Every time she looked at Fox, her heart felt as if it would tear out of her chest. *May I stay in touch with you as I work with this site?* she asked.

Of course. Fox wanted nothing more than to be here with her. To absorb her ephemeral beauty and hear her speak once more.

Aella's spirit lifted. What *was* this strange connection between them? Her curiosity was strong, but she had more pressing matters. In the next few days, Aella knew her life would change forever. How, she had no idea....

*Look for REUNION
by USA TODAY bestselling author
Lindsay McKenna,
available April 2010,
only from Silhouette® Nocturne™.*

HARLEQUIN® *Romance*®

ROMANCE, RIVALRY
AND A FAMILY REUNITED

THE BRIDES
of
BELLA ROSA

William Valentine and his beloved wife, Lucia, live
a beautiful life together, but when his former love Rosa
and the secret family they had together resurface,
an instant rivalry is formed. Can these families
get through the past and come together as one?

Step into the world of Bella Rosa
beginning this April with

Beauty and the Reclusive Prince
by

RAYE MORGAN

Eight volumes to collect and treasure!

www.eHarlequin.com

HR17650

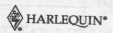

INTRIGUE

WILL THIS REUNITED FAMILY
BE STRONG ENOUGH TO EXPOSE
A LURKING KILLER?

FIND OUT IN THIS ALL-NEW
THRILLING TRILOGY FROM TOP
HARLEQUIN INTRIGUE AUTHOR

B.J. DANIELS

WHITEHORSE MONTANA

Winchester Ranch

GUN-SHY BRIDE—*April 2010*

HITCHED—*May 2010*

TWELVE-GAUGE GUARDIAN—
June 2010

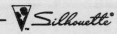